"Why didn't you tell me you were being stalked?" Max asked.

"Because I didn't know for sure," Tara said. "I didn't really believe it, until I saw...my dog."

Max stared at her intently for a long moment, then leaned his hips back against her kitchen counter and crossed his arms over his chest. "You have fifteen minutes to pack."

"What?" She stared back at him.

"Tara, I'm not leaving you here alone with some stalker on the loose. I'll find a safe haven."

Admittedly, the idea held some appeal. She'd be closer to the hospital, able to keep an eye on Max's sister. And if she stubbornly insisted on staying in her house, she doubted she'd get any sleep. She'd lie awake, frighteningly aware of every sound.

But going with Max would be a risk, too. She was already feeling too close to him. Too grateful for his protection.

LAURA SCOTT

grew up reading faith-based romance books by Grace Livingston Hill, but as much as she loved the stories, she longed for a bit more mystery and suspense. She is honored to write for the Love Inspired Suspense line at Steeple Hill Books, where a reader can find a heartwarming journey of faith amidst the thrilling danger.

Laura lives with her husband of twenty-five years and has two children, a daughter and a son, who are both in college. She works as a critical care nurse during the day at a large level-one trauma center in Milwaukee, Wisconsin, and spends her spare time writing romance.

Please visit Laura at www.laurascottbooks.com as she loves to hear from her readers.

The Thanksgiving Target

Laura Scott

Steeple
Hill®

Published by Steeple Hill Books™

STEEPLE HILL BOOKS

Steeple
Hill®

Recycling programs
for this product may
not exist in your area.

ISBN-13: 978-0-373-44364-2

THE THANKSGIVING TARGET

www.SteepleHill.com

Printed in U.S.A.

In my distress I called to the Lord; I cried to my God for help. From His temple He heard my voice; my cry came before Him, into His ears.

—*Psalms* 18:6

To my husband, Scott, with love—thanks for a truly blessed twenty-five years of marriage. I look forward to many more cherished years together!

ONE

"Wait a minute. Stop right there," a female vice commanded. "Who let you in?"

Lieutenant's Max Forrester's head snapped up, and he belatedly realized there was a woman at his sister Lissa's hospital bedside. A chair with a discarded blanket on the seat was tucked in the corner where she must have been sitting.

Who was she? The ICU clerk had told him Lissa's visitors were restricted.

"Are you Gary?" she asked sharply, a dark scowl marring her otherwise dainty features. She was young, about Lissa's age, her long dark hair pulled back in a braid that hung down to her shoulders. She was dressed in a conservative navy blue jacket and skirt, with an official-looking ID pinned to her lapel. Her radiating anger caught him off guard. "Don't you dare touch her."

Gary? Who was she talking about? He lifted his hands palm forward, hoping to calm her down. "I'm not Gary. I'm Lissa's brother, Max Forrester. The woman at the desk checked my ID before letting me in."

"Her brother?" The petite woman eyed him suspiciously, not giving him an inch. "Melissa didn't mention a brother."

She hadn't? The news hurt. Why hadn't Lissa said anything about him? True, they didn't chat often, but she'd been happy to know he was coming home on leave to spend the Thanksgiving holiday together.

Glancing down at his sister, with her bruised and battered face, he realized this woman, who must be a friend of Lissa's, had every right to be suspicious. His heart squeezed painfully in his chest. Lissa couldn't even breathe on her own because she wasn't conscious. His sister must have been mugged to end up here like this.

"Here's my ID," he said, handing it to her. "I've been in Iraq the past three years and just arrived home on leave today. When Lissa didn't meet me at the airport, I went to her apartment and her landlord told me she was here."

The woman stared at his ID for a long moment, then handed it back with a weary sigh. "I'm sorry. I should have known Gary wouldn't go so far as to disguise himself in army fatigues."

"Who are you?" Max asked, putting his ID back in his wallet. "And who's Gary?"

"My name is Tara Carmichael. I'm Melissa's social worker." She crossed her arms over her chest and gazed down at Lissa, with sorrow and despair. "Unfortunately, Gary is the man who did this to her."

Tara Carmichael eyed the handsome stranger warily. Melissa's brother cut an impressive figure in his camouflage fatigues, and she imagined he'd be even more so in action. Right now though, his tormented gaze was riveted on his sister, his face drawn into harsh lines of anger.

"What's Gary's last name?" he asked, his low voice vibrating with suppressed anger. "Where can I find him?"

She suppressed a sigh. "I wish I knew. Melissa never told me his full name. In fact, the last time she left him, she refused to go to the police to press charges. Even when I drove her to a women's shelter, she stayed for only a few days before going back home."

"What?" Max whirled on her, pinning her with his stark gaze. "Are you telling me this happened before?"

She swallowed hard, knowing his anger wasn't directed at her. Besides, she had to admit, he was showing remarkable control. "Yes, I'm afraid so. Not this bad, just a few bruises but enough to make me concerned."

He was silent, and she watched a myriad of emotions playing across his features: fury, despair, agony, helplessness. Finally he turned away, letting out a harsh sound as he tightened his fingers around the side rail of Melissa's bed. His tortured expression of self-recrimination tugged at her heart. "I didn't know," he murmured, his tone full of anguish. "I honestly didn't know."

Tara wasn't sure what to say. Melissa had obviously kept secrets. From both of them.

"She didn't mention Gary or that she had a new boyfriend?" she asked, hesitantly. It did seem odd to her that Melissa hadn't mentioned her brother during any of their meetings. Although maybe it was because he was so far away, stationed in Iraq, Melissa hadn't seen him as a true support system.

For a long moment, Lieutenant Forrester stared down at his hands. "A few months ago, she did mention meeting a guy but didn't really say much about it. I don't always have a chance to respond to e-mails, especially once the fighting heats up. Weeks can pass before I'm able to return messages."

She could only imagine how difficult it must be for the men and women who fight overseas. Even if Melissa had mentioned Gary, what would it matter? The damage was already done. Clearly, this time Gary had gone too far.

"I understand." She tried to smile, but it wasn't easy. Melissa's situation was grim. When the hospital had called, letting her know about Melissa's admission and suspected abuse, she'd immediately rushed over. Seeing Melissa in such bad shape had shaken her. Especially when Melissa had begged for her to keep Gary away, right before she'd slipped into a coma. There wasn't much she could do at that point, other than pray for her safe recovery. But sitting there, watching Melissa fight for her life, she'd vowed to stay close, supporting Melissa's escape from her boyfriend once and for all.

At least having Lieutenant Forrester here eased one of her concerns. Melissa wasn't alone, not any longer. Between her brother and herself, she was convinced they could pull Melissa through this crisis.

"You're Lissa's social worker?" he asked, breaking into her thoughts. "That's why you were allowed in?"

She hesitated, knowing she couldn't tell him much about Melissa's history of substance abuse without breaking her client's confidentiality, before nodding. "Yes. The hospital called me when she was admitted."

"I see." Max Forrester stood ramrod straight, his military bearing ingrained to the point she wondered if he ever relaxed. A spurt of sympathy nudged her heart. This couldn't be a very nice homecoming for him. After fighting for three years in Iraq, coming home to find his sister in the ICU had to be a shock.

"Have you spoken to Melissa's nurse?" she asked, wishing there was more she could do to help him.

"Not yet."

"I'll get her for you." Grateful for something constructive to do, she stepped out into the hallway, glancing around for Natalie, the young woman taking care of Melissa. Natalie was in by another patient, but as soon as she saw Tara hovering there, she finished what she was doing and stepped out. "Do you need something?"

"Melissa's brother is here, having just arrived home from Iraq, and he would like some information on Melissa's injuries."

"Sure. I'll be right in."

Tara returned to Melissa's room, and Natalie followed a few moments later. She introduced herself to Lieutenant Forrester.

"Melissa has two cracked ribs and a fairly serious head injury. The doctors have ordered another CT scan of her head for first thing in the morning, which should tell us if the injury is getting worse or better."

The lieutenant paled. "Will she wake up?"

Natalie offered a gentle smile. "So far her head injury is serious, but if it doesn't get much worse, she should recover just fine. I wish I could tell you more, but right now we can only wait and see how things go."

He swallowed hard. "Thank you." He looked so grim, his face drawn into harsh lines, that Tara had the insane urge to step closer and take his hand, offering him her support. But she kept her hands tightly clasped in front of her.

"I'll need your contact information," Natalie said, picking up a clipboard. "Have you spoken to the police yet?"

"No. But I'd like to," Max said.

Tara was surprised to hear the police were involved this time. "Do they have Gary in custody?" she asked.

"I don't think so," Natalie said with a tiny frown. "Officer James Newton gave me his card and asked me to call him when Melissa woke up so he could question her." She turned to Max. "What's your phone number?"

She wrote the information as Max rattled it off. "Can I have the police number, too?" he asked.

"I don't see why not." Natalie gave him the information and then glanced up when a shrill beeping echoed from across the hall. "Excuse me," she murmured before dashing away.

With a grim expression, Max tucked the phone number into the pocket of his camouflage shirt. Silence hung heavily between them.

Smoothing her hands over her wrinkled jacket,

Tara glanced at him. "Well, it's late and I really need to get home. But I'll be back in the morning to check on your sister."

He stared down at Melissa. "I'll stay here."

She sensed his exhaustion and understood the desire to stay near his sister, but it was obvious that he needed some rest. Her social worker training kicked in. "Lieutenant, you should really find a hotel nearby to spend the night. Melissa is in good hands. The nurses here are wonderful. We've limited her visitors to protect her. You need your rest, too. She's going to need your strength and support over the long haul."

He remained silent, but she could see the emotional tug of war on his face. "Maybe you're right," he admitted finally. "I've been on a plane since yesterday. Are there cheap hotels nearby?" His troubled gaze cut back to his sister. "I'd like to be close, keeping in touch regarding Lissa's progress."

"Of course." Tara folded away her own problems and concerns, trying to remember which hotels offered the best prices. "The family center has brochures for all the nearby hotels, and I'm pretty certain a few offer discounts for families with loved ones here at the hospital."

"That would be great." He smiled, and she was struck by how his harsh features softened with the gesture. His eyes were the same bright green as Melissa's. With his broad shoulders and chocolate-brown hair cut military short, Lieutenant Forrester was a very handsome man.

The realization made her stomach clench, sending

her back a step. How could she notice Melissa's brother in that way? She'd loved Ted, her husband, with her whole heart and soul. Her love hadn't changed when he died. She'd vowed to love him forever.

"It's no problem." She worked hard to ensure her tone portrayed only the utmost professionalism. Turning, she led the way out of the ICU, taking the elevator back down to the main level, acutely aware of Max walking silently at her side.

She found the brochures in the family center, quickly pointing out several options before leaving. She needed some distance from the tall, handsome stranger. The bus stop was right outside the main doors of the hospital, so she walked in that direction.

Remembering why she was forced to take the bus, rather than her car, made her shiver as she stepped outside. When she'd left for work earlier that evening, she'd discovered someone had maliciously slashed all four of her tires, rendering her car useless. She'd called the police and waited while they dusted for fingerprints. Since she was in a hurry to see Melissa, she'd left her disabled car in the parking lot and had taken the bus to the hospital, rather than deal with the hassle of getting her car towed.

She couldn't help wonder if the man with the navy blue jacket and baseball cap who'd followed her the other day was the same person who'd slashed her tires. His baseball cap had been pulled low over his eyes, and the collar of his jacket was pulled up to cover his face so she hadn't gotten a good look at him.

Now that it was so late, she couldn't help but glance

around, searching for anyone wearing a baseball cap as she made her way to the bus stop.

The shelter outside the bus stop wasn't deserted, as she'd hoped. There were two men standing there—neither wore a baseball cap—but one of them looked extremely disheveled, taking deep drags off a cigarette despite the signs declaring the area as nonsmoking. Her steps slowed as she hesitantly approached, and she glanced up the street hoping the bus would arrive soon. After her tire-slashing incident, it was difficult not to look at everyone around her with uncertainty.

She gathered her courage and lifted her gaze heavenward. *Please, Lord, keep me safe.*

Crossing her arms over her chest, she did her best to remain warm in spite of the chilly night temperatures. She didn't have her coat; she'd left her office in such a hurry she'd forgotten it.

"Ms. Carmichael?"

The sound of her name had her spinning around in a rush, her heart thumping in her throat. Lieutenant Max Forrester stood a few feet behind her, his face etched in a deep scowl.

"Oh, no, did something happen to Melissa?" Fearing the worst, she took several steps toward him. "Is she…?"

He held up a hand. "No, she's fine. Not fine, but her condition is unchanged."

Relief flooded her. "You had me worried."

"Ma'am, why are you out here waiting for the bus?" He swept a gaze behind her, noticing the two men sharing the bus stop with her. "It's late, half past nine at night. You'd be much safer in a taxi."

Her pride was stung by his somewhat condescending tone. She welcomed the surge of annoyance. Obviously if she'd wanted to take a taxi she would have. Maybe she didn't normally take the bus, but she wasn't about to tell this stranger her problems with vandalism. "Thanks for your concern, Lieutenant, but I can take care of myself."

"Ma'am, I'm sure you can, but since I grew up in St. Louis, I know the crime rate isn't something to brag about."

"I grew up here, too, so I'm well aware of the crime rate."

The fact they had something so minor in common shouldn't have made a difference, but she couldn't help feel a sense of kinship with Melissa's brother.

"Fine." He gave her a brisk nod that was more like a salute, widened his stance and crossed his arms over his broad chest, reminding her of a human shield. "If you're going to ride the bus home alone, I'll ride along with you."

TWO

Her jaw dropped, and she gaped at him in surprise. While she appreciated his gallantry, his protection wasn't necessary. There was no reason for her to spend any more time with him. Besides, he needed to stick close to the hospital for Melissa. "I thought you wanted to stay in one of the hotels nearby? There's no need to go out of your way."

"I'll find a hotel room on the way back. There's no rush." He frowned, and his voice grew soft and slightly grim as he added, "Lissa's not going anywhere. As you said earlier, she's in good hands."

Biting her lip, she pondered her choices. If she simply gave in and took a cab, she knew the lieutenant would step back and go about his own business. If she stubbornly took the bus, she had no doubt he'd ride along with her.

Trying to hide a shiver, she turned away, reaching into her purse to subtly check her pocketbook. She hadn't spent any money on lunch, having packed some leftovers from home, but she had filled up her gas tank earlier in the week. She didn't think there was much cash left and verified the dismal amount rather quickly. With a sigh, she closed her purse with a quiet snap.

There was no choice but to strengthen her resolve and take the bus home. Borrowing money from the stranger would be much worse than enduring a protective shadow on her ride. If the lieutenant wanted to ride the bus she couldn't stop him. Besides, she didn't have the energy to fight.

A heavy fabric dropped over her shoulders, carrying the enticing, musky scent of man. Startled, she glanced up at Max, who was straightening the camouflage jacket over her shoulders.

"You were shivering," he stated in a matter-of-fact tone, dropping his hands and refastening his duffel bag. "And I appreciate your help in lightening my load."

She wanted to smile at how he'd tried to make her believe she was really the one helping him, but sudden tears pricked her eyes. When was the last time anyone had noticed if she was tired, hungry or cold? Ridiculous to so grateful for a chivalrous gesture, and she swiped the moisture away with an impatient hand trying to pull herself together.

"Thank you, but I really wish you wouldn't do this," she told him. "I hate taking you out of your way."

In that instant, the bus lumbered up to the stop. With a sigh, she took her place behind the man who'd been smoking, grimacing a bit when he tossed his cigarette butt directly in front of her before he boarded the bus. There weren't many occupants at this time of the night, and most of them were men. One passenger wore a baseball cap backward on his head, but he looked too young to be the man she'd seen following her.

She slipped into an empty pair of seats taking the one closest to the window, not at all surprised when Max chose the seat right next to her. His broad shoulders brushed lightly against hers, and she found she was grateful for his reassuringly protective presence.

Safe. For the first time in three weeks, her underlying sense of fear melted away. If anyone was following her, he'd certainly think twice about approaching her now.

And for that small favor, she owed Lieutenant Forrester a huge debt of gratitude.

Max tried to ignore the rumbling in his stomach and slid a sideways glance at Ms. Carmichael, hoping she hadn't heard the betraying sound.

He'd stop for something to eat after he'd seen her home.

Just then, her stomach let out a low gurgle, a grumbling sound that was even louder than his.

She blushed and let out a small chuckle. "Sorry, I guess I'm hungry. I skipped dinner."

Max stared at her, realizing with a start how pretty she was. Her cheekbones were high, her skin translucent. In his anxiety over Lissa he hadn't really noticed her mesmerizing blue eyes. Not that he had time to think about a pretty woman, especially since he needed to get back to the hospital to see Lissa. Even taking this much time away bothered him, but he couldn't ignore

Tara's plight, either. Besides, he planned to be there for his sister, offering strength and support for the duration of his leave.

He didn't want to think about what would happen once he returned to Iraq.

This wasn't the time to worry about the future. Right now he was hungry. He'd already figured out that Tara didn't have much money, especially when she'd subtly checked her purse for cab money.

They were both hungry and needed to eat.

"I haven't eaten in several hours myself. I don't mean to be presumptuous, but seeing as this is my first night on American soil in three years, would you do me the honor of allowing me to buy you dinner?" He couldn't help but produce a wistful smile. Did she have any idea how much he'd looked forward to his first American meal? The food they'd given them on the plane hadn't counted, since he could barely recognize what it was. "It's no fun eating alone."

"That's a kind offer, but…" Her voice trailed off, and he noticed she shifted uncomfortably in her seat. He was mentally prepared for her refusal when all of a sudden she abruptly nodded. "You're right. It's no fun eating alone. You've come a long way home, Lieutenant, after dutifully serving our country. I'd be happy to share dinner with you."

"Really?" He couldn't hide his surprise. Maybe she was simply taking pity on a lonely soldier, but he wasn't going to argue. He was thrilled she'd agreed to accompany him. He'd hoped to eat with Lissa, but this was almost just as nice. "Great. Is there someplace we can go that's close to your home? The only restaurant I'm familiar with is the one where Lissa works as a waitress."

Tara tilted her head, regarding him thoughtfully. "I know where your sister works. It's not far from Maplewood, where I live. And I happen to know they serve meals late, including breakfast if you're in the mood."

"Breakfast would be great, but I think I'm going to have a large juicy American burger slathered with the works," he mused. A glance out the window confirmed they were close to the restaurant. "Let's get off here then, if you don't mind."

"Not at all." She stood, clutching his camouflage jacket closer to her shoulders. He was glad she'd stopped shivering. Taking a step back, he gestured for her to move out in front of him.

The walk to the restaurant from the bus stop didn't take long. Tara glanced at his duffel, as if worried it might be too heavy for him to lug around, which made him smile. He'd hauled his own gear over many a mile before, riding around the city in the comfort of a bus didn't even come close to being a burden.

They took opposite seats at a booth. He opened the menu, marveling at the selection, but in the end, he didn't change his mind about what he wanted. Tara ordered a chicken breast sandwich, and once the waiter left, he took a healthy gulp of his water, enjoying the icy smoothness against his parched throat.

Even the water tasted good.

"Lieutenant, tell me, how long will you be staying in St. Louis?" Tara asked.

"Please, call me Max. I'm home for just a twenty-day leave, but my tour of duty ends in another year. After that, I'll have to decide whether I'll reenlist or go back to the private sector." Not that he had any clue as to what he'd do once he was out. The army had quickly become his life, and his men had become his brothers. He'd lost his best friend, who had died in his arms shortly after their deployment to Iraq, but even that tragedy couldn't break the bonds he had with the rest of his men.

But his sister obviously needed him, too. More than he'd realized.

"Reenlist?" Tara's big blue eyes widened. "I'm surprised you're even considering another tour of duty. You've put in your time in Iraq, haven't you?"

"Yes." He finished his water and placed the empty glass toward the edge of the table, hoping someone would refill it for him. "But there is still a lot of work to be done there. To be honest, my decision was going to depend on Lissa." His mouth tightened as he thought of his sister.

"Have you called the police officer assigned to her case yet?" she asked.

Max nodded. "I left him a message. I guess he works the day shift."

"I'm really glad you're here for Melissa," Tara admitted, sitting back in her seat with a sigh. "And I'm relieved to know the police are involved. Gary needs to be arrested for what he's done, and this time, I don't think Melissa will be able to protect him."

He scowled, wondering again why Lissa had even gotten mixed up with someone who'd hurt her. He simply couldn't understand it. He and Lissa had been raised Christian, but maybe Lissa had fallen away from the church, just like he had. Losing Keith had made it impossible to maintain his faith. What had caused Lissa to lose hers? He shook off the depressing thoughts. "I'll take care of her, don't worry. I'll move in with her and refuse to leave until he's safe behind bars."

She laughed, a light musical sound that tightened his stomach in awareness. "Sounds like a great plan to me."

Their food arrived promptly, diverting his attention from Tara. His mouth literally watered at the wonderful scent of his burger and fries, and he hoped he wasn't being too much of a pig as he heartily dug in to his meal.

Tara didn't seem to mind. She was enjoying her grilled chicken just as much. "This is delicious. Thanks for inviting me," she said between bites.

He knew he was the lucky one, sharing this meal with her. He wanted to savor the food and the time with Tara, drawing them out for as long as possible. But she was nearly finished, so he polished off the rest of his burger quickly.

"Are you up for dessert?" he asked hopefully.

She shook her head with an amused grimace. "Sorry, nothing for me, thanks. I need to get home. My poor dog is going to be sitting at the door wondering where I am."

He understood she didn't want to linger and signaled for the waiter to bring the bill. "What kind of dog do you have?"

"A cute little Westie. A West Highland white terrier," she clarified at his puzzled look. "His name is Beau. I rescued him from the local shelter a couple years ago."

"Well then, let's not keep Beau waiting, especially if he's been home alone all day." He paid for the meal with cash, and thinking of Melissa living off her tips, he left a hefty sum.

"Well, I do have a neighbor lady, Mrs. Henderson, who comes over to let him out at lunchtime for me. She has a key and lets him out in the early evening too if I'm working late," Tara said over her shoulder as they left the restaurant.

"Which way to your house?" he asked, feeling much better with food in his belly. Now if only Lissa would get well, he'd be happy. Or at least content. Was it selfish of him to want her home from the hospital in time for Thanksgiving? Maybe. "Should we walk, or do we need to catch another bus?"

"We can walk. It's only about six or seven blocks from here." She headed off in the opposite direction from where Lissa's apartment building was located. She stopped and glanced at him. "If you'd rather head back to the hospital, I'd certainly understand."

"Ma'am, it might be only six or seven blocks but it's

ten-thirty at night. I'll walk you home. There's no way in the world I'm leaving you alone at this hour."

"If you want me to call you Max, then you should probably stop calling me ma'am," she pointed out, as they headed down the street. "You're making me feel old."

"Old?" he chuckled, a rusty sound even to his own ears. "You're young, probably the same age as my sister."

She arched a brow at him. "I'm a couple years older than Melissa," she corrected in a prim tone.

"Still very young." Especially when lately he'd felt as if he were a hundred years old. Maybe in part because he'd seen things no man should have to endure. Despite the hardships, he firmly believed freedom was worth the effort.

Tara set a brisk pace, and he wasn't sure it was because she was cold or because she was anxious to get rid of him. He couldn't blame her if she felt uncomfortable being in the dark alone with him. After they walked several blocks she lifted her hand and pointed. "My house is over there, the third one from the corner."

"The little red brick house with the white trim and black shutters?" he asked.

"Yes." As they approached, she frowned. "I wonder why Beau isn't barking his head off by now. Usually he hears me coming long before this."

An icy chill snaked down his spine, and he grasped her arm. "Tara, wait. Maybe I should go up first."

Tuning in to his abrupt wariness, she sucked in a

quick breath. "Why? You think something happened to Beau?"

He couldn't explain his trepidation, and he held on to her arm, bringing her to a halt. "Give me your key," he commanded.

She handed it over, and he swept a glance over the area, making sure no one was lurking around.

He put the key in the lock and turned the doorknob, slowly pushing the door open. The house was eerily silent. From where he stood outside, he stretched until he could slide his hand over the inside wall of her foyer, seeking the light switch.

"Stay here." The area flooded with light, and he wasn't sure if it was a good sign or a bad sign that the dog wasn't lying there on the floor directly in front of the door.

"No way. I'm coming with you."

He wanted to argue, but then he heard it—a little whimper of sound.

"Beau?" Tara must have heard it, too, and she pushed past him, rushing down the hall into the kitchen, with blatant disregard of her own safety.

"Wait!" He grit his teeth with anger and followed, intent on keeping her out of harm's way.

"Oh, no. Beau!"

When he rounded the corner, he saw what had caused her cry of distress. Beau was lying on his side— obviously sick, unable lift his white, fluffy head off the floor.

"Beau?" Feeling helpless, he watched Tara anxiously kneel beside her dog, gently gathering his limp body into her arms. She cradled him against her chest, nuzzling his head with her face as she stood. "What happened? Are you sick?"

"Here, let me take a look at him."

She obviously didn't want to let Beau go, so Max simply placed his large palm over the dog's chest to check his pulse, relieved to feel the thready, irregular beat. "I think we need to get him to a vet as soon as possible."

"The emergency clinic isn't far." Tara took a step toward the door but then stopped, her expression stricken. "I don't have my car."

No car. And a ride on the bus would take too long, if they even allowed a dog on the city bus. He quickly considered their options. "Does Mrs. Henderson have a car?"

"Yes." Tara looked relieved and instantly rushed outside, headed straight for the house to the right, a robin's egg–blue Cape Cod. She lifted her hand and pounded on the door.

After what seemed like a long time, the door was opened by a squat, round woman wearing thick glasses and a bright purple fuzzy robe. "Tara? What is it?"

"Beau is sick. My car has a flat tire, so will you let me borrow yours to take him to the vet?" Tara spoke loudly, making Max suspect Mrs. Henderson didn't hear too well, and clutched the dog close to her breast as if it were her child. Max understood Beau was important to her. "Please? I promise to bring it back soon."

"Sure, but what happened?" The woman opened her door and gestured for them to come in. "Beau was fine when I let him out about an hour ago."

"I don't know. Maybe he ate something that made him sick." Tara looked impatient, and Mrs. Henderson must have noticed because she hurried over to her purse and dug out her car keys. Tara snatched them from her grasp. "Thank you so much. I'll reimburse you for the gas."

"Don't worry about it. Just take good care of Beau." The woman's expression was one of concern.

Tara nodded. He reached over and took the keys from her. "Why don't you let me drive?"

She didn't argue and hurried out to the garage to Mrs. Henderson's large, ancient green Buick. He closed the passenger door behind her and then hustled around to the driver's side. He backed carefully out of the driveway. "Which way?"

"To the right, then left at the corner." Tara gave him directions, dividing her attention between the road and her dog.

Her love and worry for her pet was obvious. He assumed she lived in the house alone with only Beau as a companion. The news that Tara might not have a man in her life made him secretly relieved; yet he knew it shouldn't matter. Not when her dog was sick and his sister barely clung to her life in the ICU.

This wasn't the time to think about the pretty social worker on a personal level. Hadn't he learned his lesson before? He'd discovered the hard way that gratitude wasn't the path to finding love and commitment. Besides, his future wasn't his own; he'd be back in Iraq before long. He pushed the inappropriate thoughts of Tara away and centered his attention on the road.

"There, on the right. That's the emergency vet."

He saw the building she indicated and pulled into the driveway. He'd barely pulled the Buick to a stop when she jumped out of the car.

"Wait," he called, but she disappeared behind the glass doors without a backward glance. He sat there, wondering why he was here at the vet when he should be at the hospital sitting beside Lissa. His sister should be his highest priority.

Yet he couldn't simply abandon Tara. Not until he knew her dog was okay. She'd supported Lissa at the hospital, had tried to help his sister in the past, too. Tara deserved at least a little support.

Besides, he'd left his duffel bag on the floor of her foyer, so he'd have to go back there anyway. Rubbing the exhaustion from his face, he turned off the car and walked into the building.

Tara and Beau were already in the back, seeing the vet. Watching them in deep conversation made him hesitate, but then he decided he'd barged into her life this much, he may as well go for broke. He approached the desk. "I'm with Tara and her dog, Beau."

"Oh, sure. Come on back." The secretary/receptionist buzzed him through, and he found Tara, her blue eyes luminous with tears.

"I don't understand how this could have happened,"

she was saying in a low husky tone. "My neighbor Mrs. Henderson lets him outside for me, but she wouldn't hurt him. And I don't think she takes him out of the area between our yards. Are you sure he couldn't have simply eaten something bad? Something poisonous to dogs?"

"I'm sure." The vet was an older man with a kind, gentle expression. "Leave him with me, and I'll have him fixed up just fine in a few days. You can call to check on him anytime."

Tara didn't say anything for several long minutes but then swiped more tears from her face as she nodded. "All right. Please take good care of him for me."

"I will," the vet promised.

She turned and nearly stumbled into him. Max lightly grasped her shoulders, holding her steady. "Tara? What is it? What happened to Beau?"

"He was given some sort of sedative," she whispered, her voice strained to the point of nearly breaking. "The vet believes someone drugged him on purpose."

THREE

Numb from the top of her head to the tips of her toes, Tara sat beside Max in the car, her throat thick with overwhelming sorrow. She'd almost lost Beau. Her poor little puppy. Beau wasn't exactly a puppy, since she'd gotten him from the shelter a few years ago, but he was so cute and still a puppy at heart. He'd always be her puppy, full of fun and energy, constantly happy to see her.

Her eyes filled again. Beau had helped keep her grounded after Ted died. She didn't know what she'd do without him. Beau just had to survive. She closed her eyes and silently prayed that God would allow Beau to recover quickly.

It took her a few minutes to realize Max had stopped the car and was looking at her expectantly. She glanced outside, realizing with a start they were home.

Or at least at Mrs. Henderson's house.

"Tara? Are you okay?"

She shook her head but opened the car door and climbed out. Max moved fast. He met her before she could get too far. "Don't go home yet," he said, capturing her arm. "Not without me. Give me a minute to return Mrs. Henderson's car keys."

It was easier to obey than to think. She nodded.

Standing on the narrow grass lawn between her house and Mrs. Henderson's, she shivered and clutched Max's camouflage jacket tighter around her shoulders. Beau had looked so sick. She missed him already.

"Tara, I'm going to go through your house. Wait outside for me."

She gave another weary nod as she huddled beneath his jacket. She couldn't even imagine what Max might find. Yet she also couldn't imagine why anyone would try to hurt Beau, either.

"You can come in now. There's no one here. But I do want you to take a look around, to see if anything looks out of place."

Reluctantly, she mounted the steps and headed inside to meet him. Trying to tell herself she was being ridiculous, she started in the living room, seeing nothing unusual, before heading into the kitchen where she'd found Beau. His food and water bowls were empty; she only fed him once a day in the morning. Max stood silently off to the side as she gazed around.

"Everything seems fine," she said, helplessly lifting her shoulders. "I don't see anything wrong."

"Okay, but double-check the bathroom and bedrooms too, just to make certain. I'll take another quick look outside and then meet you back here."

She did as Max asked, but there too, everything seemed to be the way she'd left it. She was a neat person by nature, and nothing was amiss. In her room, she collapsed on the side of her bed for a moment, suddenly exhausted. Her feet ached, and she longed to change into more comfortable clothes. She still felt numb, but some of the effect was beginning to wear off. As much as she wanted nothing more than to crawl into bed and pull a pillow over her head to forget all the troubles of her day, she forced herself to stand and return to meet Max in the kitchen.

His face was somber and she instantly asked, "What's wrong?"

"I found this outside in the backyard, at the base of your small maple tree." He gestured to a shredded fast-food wrapper with less than half a hamburger inside. "Somehow, given how neat and tidy your home is, I doubt you left it out there."

No, she hadn't. Her mouth went dry, and she swallowed hard, understanding why he'd looked so serious. "You think the vet is right? Someone hid some drugs in the sandwich and left it for Beau?"

"I think it's possible. Call the police." His voice held the unmistakable tone of a command. "I'm sure they can test what's left of this for potential drug residue."

The police. They already knew about her tire-slashing episode. What would they think now? At first, when she'd thought someone was following her, they hadn't been too concerned. But then finding her car with all four tires slashed, she'd garnered more attention. And now poor Beau.

Why? How could this happen? What had she done

to become someone's target? She supposed she should be glad that Max had found the fast-food wrapper outside, which might indicate that whoever had tried to harm Beau hadn't been inside her house.

Yet she still felt very alone and far too vulnerable.

"Tara?" Max's expression now held concern. "Are you all right? Did you hear me? Beau will be fine, but you need to call the police."

"I heard you." She pulled herself together with an effort. She didn't like taking orders from Max, but she couldn't afford not to call the police, either. "I will. Thanks for following me home. I don't know what I would have done without you. But I know you're worried about Melissa. I don't want you to feel as if you need to hang around. I'll be fine."

He hesitated, and she suspected he realized she was kindly trying to get rid of him. She didn't think Max was the type to push his company on anyone—the way he'd so nicely asked her to dinner proved that. But he had insisted on following her home on the bus. He was the type of man who clearly took his role as protector very seriously.

He was only being nice, yet she suddenly felt very guilty for inviting him into the home she'd shared with her husband.

"Tara, I'd really rather wait until the police arrive. What if whoever did this is still hanging around somewhere close by?"

She bit her lip, wondering what to do. If she allowed Max to stay, then he'd end up hearing the whole story of what had been happening to her. And as much as she appreciated everything he'd done for her up until this point, she didn't want to burden him with her problems.

She couldn't help but glance toward her kitchen window over the sink, the one that overlooked her backyard. The image of the man with a ball cap following her as she went out for lunch last week rushed to the forefront of her mind. Was he the one who'd done the damage to her car tires? If she told Max about the guy, he would for sure refuse to leave. The memory of the man made her clench her fists, frightened to be alone.

This indecisiveness wasn't like her. She needed to pull herself together, to create some sort of plan. Max was right. She absolutely needed to report this new development to the police. "Okay, you can stay for a bit." She went to the phone and dialed the nonemergency St. Louis P.D. number that she now knew by heart. "Once I'm finished, I'll make coffee."

But Max was already shaking his head, making his way to the counter on the opposite side of the kitchen where her coffeemaker was located. "No, I'll do it. You've had a rough day. Sit down. I'll take care of everything."

As before, his thoughtfulness brought a lump to her throat. How did his kindness manage to touch her so deeply? She didn't want to think about Max, so she focused her attention on trying to fix her problems instead.

After giving the dispatcher on the other end of the line

her information, she hung up and did as Max suggested, sitting down to put her feet up. She watched him working in her kitchen, realizing she was in danger of becoming too accustomed to Max's calm, reassuring presence.

He was Melissa's brother, here to look after his sister, not her. He was home for only a few weeks.

She'd learned a long time ago that it was better to stand on her own two feet rather than to lean on someone else. And despite how Max suddenly seemed to make himself at home in her house, she knew full well it would only be a matter of time before she'd be alone again.

The police arrived on her doorstep mere minutes after she'd placed the call. Either they were having a slow night or the police file on her had grown so thick she warranted a high-level response.

She found herself hoping for the former reason. The latter would indicate she had every reason to be afraid.

The two officers introduced themselves as Officer Anderson and Officer Schimberg. Officer Anderson was tall and thin, while Officer Schimberg was short and stout.

They asked her endless questions, going over the events again step-by-step. They walked through her house and then went outside to look around her back yard. As Max predicted, they took the food wrapper and the remains of the hamburger and promised to test it for residue.

"Ms. Carmichael, it's highly likely these events, the man following you, the tire slashing and this possible drugging of your dog have all been done by the same perpetrator," Officer Anderson said with a serious frown.

"Yes, I know." From the corner of her eye, she caught Max's scowl as he listened, but thankfully he didn't interrupt.

"Are you sure you can't give us a better idea who to look for? Some guy you've jilted?" Officer Schimberg asked. "Anyone at work that might have held a grudge against you?"

"I told you before that I'm not seeing anyone. My husband passed away just a little over a year and a half ago. Many of my clients aren't happy with me, but I can't think of anyone who would do something like this."

"Which client has been the most unhappy with you lately?" Officer Anderson persisted.

She hesitated and then reluctantly admitted, "Tyrone Adams." As much as she didn't want to think Tyrone was capable of such cruelty, the young man was a different person under the influence of drugs. Could the mystery man with the blue baseball hat be Tyrone? She hadn't gotten a good look at him to be sure.

"We'll have a chat with Tyrone," Officer Anderson said, looking happy to have at least one suspect.

"What about Lieutenant Forrester?" Officer Schimberg shot a suspicious glance at Max. "How long have you known him?"

She felt her face flush. "I only met Lieutenant Forrester tonight. His sister is a client of mine, and she's sick in the hospital."

"I just arrived home from Iraq today," Max spoke up, seemingly not offended to be considered a possible suspect for the second time that evening. "I was on the AirTran Airways flight from Germany to St. Louis, with a layover in New York. My superiors will gladly verify my story."

"Write down the name and phone number of your commanding officer, if you don't mind," Officer Anderson suggested.

Max did as requested, despite her protests.

After Max handed over the information, there was a moment of silence before the two officers exchanged a resigned look as they made their way to the door.

"Ms. Carmichael, we'll check on Tyrone, but just in case he's not the guy, you need to go through every single one of your clients, listing every possibility no matter how unlikely," Officer Anderson said in a serious tone. "Please call us once you have the list."

"I will." Tara stood and followed them to the door. "Thanks for coming."

Officer Anderson and Officer Schimberg left, and she closed the door behind them, warily turning to face Max. His expression was dark, like an impending storm.

"Why didn't you tell me you're being stalked?" he demanded, in a tone that was soft yet edged in steel at the same time.

"Because I didn't know for sure." She didn't like sounding so defensive. "I didn't really believe it, not until I saw poor Beau. Regardless, it's really none of your business, is it? Thanks for staying, but it's late and I'm tired. I'll see you at the hospital in the morning."

Her hint for him to leave was anything but subtle. He silently stared at her for a long moment and then leaned his hips back against her kitchen counter and crossed his strong arms over his chest. "You have fifteen minutes to pack a bag."

"What?" She gaped at him.

"Tara, I'm not leaving you here alone with some stalker on the loose. I'm going to find a hotel close to the hospital to spend the night, and I think it's best if you come with me." He must have read the frank panic in her eyes because he hastily added, "Not in the same room, of course. At least in a hotel you'll be safe from harm."

Admittedly, the idea held a certain appeal. Not from a financial perspective, but at least she'd be close to the hospital, able to keep an eye on Melissa. And if she stubbornly insisted on staying in her house, she doubted she'd get any sleep. She'd no doubt lie awake, frighteningly aware of every sound.

But going with Max would be a risk. She was already feeling too close to him. Too grateful for his protection.

She barely knew him.

Her silence was obviously wearing on him, since his tone grew impatient. "This guy knows where you live. He tried to get rid of your dog and probably already knows Mrs. Henderson is hard of hearing. What's to stop him from showing up in the middle of the night? He almost killed Beau. How do you know he won't feel more desperate the next time he shows up?"

A shiver racked her body, having nothing to do with the temperature outside. His words, spoken so bluntly, made the entire situation sound that much more sinister.

Max was right. She didn't know who the guy was, so how could she know what lengths he'd go to get back at her for some perceived wrong she'd committed. She would be better off in a hotel, miles from her house. She needed to think logically, not emotionally.

Ted had loved her. He'd want her to be safe.

Max pushed away from the counter, coming to stand in front of her. "Please, Tara? I don't feel right leaving you here. There must be something I can say to convince you."

She could almost hear Ted's voice telling her not to be foolish.

"I'll stay in a hotel room for tonight," she agreed slowly. "But I don't want you to feel responsible for me. This isn't your problem."

He didn't say anything in response, but as she turned to go down to her bedroom to pack an overnight bag, she suspected Max was incapable of standing aside, allowing her to face her problems on her own.

And deep down, despite her guilt over the prickly awareness she felt around Melissa's brother, she was secretly glad that she had Max to lean on, at least for a few more hours.

Max ground the heels of his hands against his eyes, trying to stay calm and rational and awake as he waited for Tara to return with her overnight case.

He couldn't remember the last time he'd met a more stubborn woman. There was a part of him that admired her strength, her ability to weather a shock such as finding her dog hurt or her tires slashed. But at the moment he was more frustrated than anything. Lissa had teased him about being a control freak and his sister might be right.

Someone was stalking Tara. Yet she'd never said a word, hadn't so much as hinted at her troubles. Most women were more than grateful for a helping hand—but not Tara. She seemed to think she could take this guy on by herself. And, like always, his need to protect others kicked in at the first sign of a woman in distress. He wanted nothing more than to keep Tara out of harm's way.

But her well-being wasn't his problem, as she'd so clearly pointed out. He wasn't responsible for her.

He should be glad she felt that way. He took a deep breath and let it out slowly in an attempt to loosen the tightness of his neck. The thought of anyone hurting Tara made his blood turn cold. Thankfully, she wasn't stupid enough to stay here by herself.

Not after someone had been at her house.

He'd help her get away from this creep stalking her, but then he needed to leave her alone. He didn't understand this intense attraction he felt for her. She was beautiful, but he'd never particularly cared about outward appearances. He appreciated her nobility in dedicating her life to helping others—people like his sister. Yet she was also a widow. She'd emphatically denied having a man in her life when the police had asked, and he understood she was clearly stating she didn't want one.

Which should be fine with him. She was a woman in trouble, and he didn't really want to be involved in her problems any more than he already was. Especially since he refused to make the same mistake again, misinterpreting gratitude and friendship for something more.

He wasn't going to be in town for long anyway. Soon, he'd be flown back to Iraq.

A twenty-day leave wasn't much time. His main concern was to find Gary, Lissa's abusive boyfriend. He was glad the police were already on the case, although until he talked to them, he wouldn't know if they were making any progress or not. And if he could give Tara a little protection from her stalker, he would. But he wouldn't allow himself to get too close.

Tara returned to the kitchen, dressed in comfortable jeans, a sweater and a heavy-duty blue denim jacket. She looked much younger in the casual clothes. The navy blue suit she'd worn earlier had given her a more professional appearance. In her arms she carried a small overnight bag and his camouflage cargo jacket.

He was ridiculously disappointed that she'd taken his jacket off to replace it with one of her own.

"Here," she said, handing the army jacket to him.

"Thanks." He took the coat and stuffed it back into his duffel. Then he plucked the overnight bag from her hands, ignoring her protest, and slung both bags over his shoulder. He stepped back so Tara could go out the door first. She threw one last glance over her shoulder, and he understood the regret darkening her eyes. Leaving her home hadn't been an easy decision.

He followed her outside and then waited until she'd closed and locked her door before they headed back down the road toward the bus stop. They hadn't quite reached the corner when a loud explosion blasted his ears, rocking the night.

In a heartbeat, he shielded Tara with his body, convinced they were back in Iraq under mortar attack.

What happened? Where was the enemy firing from?

He glanced back over his shoulder and once the flashback faded, he realized Tara's house was engulfed in smoke and flames.

Someone had tried to kill her.

FOUR

The earth shuddered beneath her feet, throwing her against Max, whose strong arms held her upright, his broad shoulders protecting her as he turned, putting himself in front of her. The explosion reverberated through her head over and over in a deafening echo. The acrid scent of smoke stung her nose.

What happened? She clung to Max's arms, twisting to search for the source of the sound, not sure what she expected to see. A burning car or truck maybe?

Flickering flames danced in the gaping hole where a corner of her house used to be. Her house. She gasped in horror, unable to tear her gaze from the awful sight.

Her house!

"Tara? Are you all right?"

She could barely hear Max through the ringing in her ears. The destruction seared painfully into her eyes, making them burn.

Her home, the home she'd shared with Ted, was gone.

Max's arms tightened around her. Dimly, she realized her knees had buckled.

Gone. Her home was gone.

Suddenly Max swept her off her feet, striding away from the wreckage. She clutched his shirt, knowing she should protest, but unable to remember why.

"Mrs. Henderson!" Her hoarse voice sounded far away, as if coming from the end of a long tunnel.

"What?" Max's steps slowed.

She forced her brain to think, to react. She pushed against him, turning awkwardly to glance behind them. "We can't leave. Not without checking on Mrs. Henderson."

He stopped, looking down at her. "No. We're too exposed out here," he said in a low, rough voice.

"Please. I can't just leave her." Sensing her distress, he set her down gently but kept a hand on her arm to keep her steady. She hadn't realized she was swaying. Pulling herself together, she tried to make him understand. "The blast was on the side of the house closest to Mrs. Henderson's. What if she fell? What if the fire spreads to her house? I can't just leave her. She's been like a grandmother to me."

His fingers tightened, and she could tell he didn't want to go. Finally he relented.

"Stay close," he ordered in a harsh tone he must have used on his men under his command. He wrapped a steel arm around her shoulders as they retraced their steps, heading back toward her neighbor's house. People were coming outside, standing and staring in horror. In the distance, she could hear the wail of sirens. "I don't like this," Max muttered. "Your stalker could be hiding anywhere."

Her stalker? It took a moment for his words to sink in to her befuddled brain. First her car, then Beau and now her house.

Her stalker wasn't just some man who was angry with her, looking for ways to get back at her, to inconvenience her, to frighten her.

Whoever this man was, he'd just blown up her house.

Tiny white dots swirled in front of her eyes, and the blood drained from her head. She bent over, bracing her hands on her knees, feeling like she might faint.

She never fainted. Ever.

There was always a first time for everything.

The idiotic thought came from nowhere. For a moment she feared she was losing her mind. She struggled to breathe, fighting a wave of darkness, and clutched a hand to her heart, seeking guidance.

Lord, I need You. Please give me strength.

"Tara? Come on, hang in there. Don't pass out on me."

"I won't." She wished she could sound more convincing, but finally she was able to take several deep breaths, pushing herself upright. "I'm fine. We need to find Mrs. Henderson."

Max's gaze clung to hers for several seconds before he glanced away. "We'll find her."

His confidence helped her to believe, and she forced herself to take several steps toward Mrs. Henderson's tiny blue house just as her neighbor, wearing the familiar bright purple robe, appeared on the doorstep.

Safe. Sweet, elderly Mrs. Henderson was safe. Her thick glasses were askew, and her tight gray curls were disheveled, but she was moving under her own power, a welcome, reassuring sight.

Dear Lord, thank You. Thank You for keeping her safe.

Relief made Tara dizzy. Max's arms tightened around her, and she sensed his attention was focused on their surroundings now that they knew Mrs. Henderson was unharmed.

"Tara?" Mrs. Henderson called, as they approached. "What happened to your house?"

"I don't know." She cast a warning glance at Max. She would not tolerate him frightening this poor woman with talk about stalkers. Gently, she took the elderly woman's hand. "Are you all right? You're not hurt?"

"I'm fine. Tumbled to the floor, but lucky for me," she said as she smiled wryly and patted her round hip, "I have enough padding to cushion these old bones."

She gently squeezed the woman's hand. "I'm so glad you're not hurt."

Fire trucks and police cars pulled up moments later, and soon her quiet, sedate, family-friendly neighborhood was overwhelmed in chaos. As the firefighters turned their hoses to the blaze, the police ushered her and Max to the closest police car to take their statements.

She'd never been inside the back of a police car before, but she was too numb to appreciate the novel experience. Max climbed in beside her, amazingly still carrying their bags, which he stuffed on the floor at their feet. Officer Anderson, the taller policeman who'd come to see her earlier that evening, slid into the front seat.

He turned around so he could look at them through the metal grate separating the front from the back. "I guess we know why your stalker drugged your dog," he said in lieu of a greeting.

She wrinkled her brow, not following his logic.

"He obviously drugged the dog so he could sneak inside her house without causing a ruckus," Max agreed in a grim tone.

"Exactly." Officer Anderson's expression was intense. "The focal point of the blast seems to be centered on the back side of the house."

"The back side?" Max echoed. "That's where the bedrooms are located."

"I'm sure he was hoping she'd be asleep when the explosion hit."

"And she would have been," Max ground out between clenched teeth, his anger palpable. "If I hadn't dragged her out."

They were talking about her as if she weren't sitting right there with them, but she couldn't find the strength to complain. Max was absolutely right. By forcing her to leave, convincing her to go to a hotel with him, he'd saved her life.

And while she'd often wondered why God had taken Ted's life, instead of hers, she discovered she was profoundly grateful.

Because she very much wanted to live.

A jackhammer pounded behind his temples, anger reverberating through his system. He was furious. At God for allowing this to happen. At Gary for hurting his sister. At the police for not finding the source of the explosion sooner, before the bomb or the gas leak or the whatever had blown Tara's house to smithereens, nearly killing them.

At himself, for not following his instinct to rip her house apart from top to bottom.

Even now, sitting with her in the cramped backseat of a squad car, he knew Tara was not safe. Her stalker was out there somewhere. The thought of such evil threatening her made his gut churn.

He wouldn't be satisfied until they were far away from her house, somewhere where this guy harboring such animosity and hatred couldn't find her.

Bands of fear tightened around his chest, making it difficult to breathe.

She'd almost died. Tara had almost *died*.

"I have to tell you, the captain isn't going to pony up police protection," Anderson warned. "Not without proof that this explosion wasn't an accident."

"Accident?" Tara's trembling voice ripped at his heart. "How could blowing up my house possibly be an accident?"

"I'm not saying I believe it was." Anderson lifted his palms up in surrender. "But there's a possibility your furnace or your stove was leaking natural gas, causing the explosion."

"Accidental explosions are rare," Max pointed out, knowing the cop's theory was ridiculous. "I didn't smell any natural gas when I was inside, and neither did you. We were walking to the bus stop when it blew. I understand the need for an investigation, but with everything else going on—the tire slashing, the dog drugging—it's obvious someone wants to hurt Tara."

And they'd very nearly succeeded.

"We haven't located Tyrone Adams yet," Anderson admitted. "Have you had time to make a list of all your clients who might hold a grudge against you?"

"No." Tara brushed a strand of hair away from her face with a shaky hand. Max took her slender fingers and gently held them in his. She didn't pull away but clung to his hand tightly. "I'm sorry, but I can't imagine Tyrone or any of my clients doing something like this. Any one of them might get angry with me, but I can honestly say they couldn't hate me enough to try to k-kill me."

The slight hitch in her voice made him want to wrap her in his arms and never let her go. The logical part of his brain reminded him she wasn't his to protect. And even if she was, support and friendship weren't a prelude for everlasting love. He shoved the logical voice aside.

It didn't matter.

He'd failed to protect Keith and Lissa. He wouldn't be able to live with himself if he failed to protect Tara, too. Keeping Tara safe was more important than insulating his heart.

"Are we finished here?" he asked Anderson. "I'd like to take Tara someplace safe."

"Where?"

Raising a brow, he pursed his lips and decided not to respond. No one needed to know where they were going, including the police.

Anderson stared at him through the metal grate for a long, hard moment. Max lifted his chin and returned the cop's glare, refusing to back down. If the police weren't going to offer protection, fine. He'd handle the task himself.

"I'll give you my cell-phone number," Tara said. "That way you can call me if you need to reach me."

He didn't even want the police to have that much information, although it was possible her cell number was somewhere in their files. Not that he really suspected someone on the force wanted to hurt her. What would be their motive? Tara was clearly a law-abiding citizen. Still, past experience taught him that not all those who promised to protect and serve took the vow seriously.

Some men thrived on violence.

"Use my cell number," he said, just to be ultra-cautious. He rattled off the number watching as Anderson wrote it in his small brown notebook.

"Got it," Anderson closed his notebook, indicating their brief interview was over. "We'll be in touch tomorrow, after the arson investigator has a chance to go through your house, pinpointing the origin of the blast."

"Thank you," Tara said quietly.

"Wait," Max said swiftly, when Anderson moved to climb out of the squad car.

The cop glanced at him questioningly.

"We need a ride to St. Louis General Hospital. I don't want to risk taking Tara away from here via public transportation."

She flashed him an odd glance, no doubt wondering why he didn't just have the cops drive them straight to the hotel, but he tightened his hand on hers, silently asking her to trust him.

There was no such thing as being too careful, not with Tara's life at stake.

"Sure. Just give me a minute to touch base with my partner."

"No problem." Max waited until Anderson climbed out of the squad car and slammed the door behind them, effectively locking them in.

"Tara, I know you're exhausted and want nothing more than to get to the hotel as quickly as possible, but I don't want to risk being followed." He tried to read the expression in her eyes by the lights reflected inside by the nearby emergency vehicles. "Humor me for a little while longer yet, okay?"

She stared down at their entwined fingers. "Okay."

She was in shock, quiet, subdued. He wished there was something he could do to bring back the stubborn, feisty woman who'd argued with him.

Within moments Anderson and his partner, Schimberg, were back, climbing into the front seat. Anderson took the wheel.

"All set?" Anderson asked, starting the police car.

"Sure." He glanced down at Tara, who didn't answer. She was turned in her seat, staring out the window at the charred remains of her house. He sensed she was barely hanging on to her composure. He wanted to hold her close, to promise to be there for her until this creep was caught and locked up behind bars.

But he couldn't make any such promise. All he could do was hope and pray the police would capture the guy stalking her before his twenty-day leave was over.

Tara held herself upright with an effort, staring sightlessly out the window as Officer Anderson drove through the night. She longed to rest her weary head on Max's broad shoulder but told herself his strong hand holding hers was enough comfort.

Poor Max. He'd certainly gotten more than he'd bargained for when he'd insisted on accompanying her home.

The image of her burning house replayed over and over in her mind until she wanted to scream with frustration. She drew a ragged breath, controlling the sense of panic.

What was wrong with her? Here she was, feeling sorry for herself over losing the home she'd shared with Ted when Melissa Forrester was right now fighting for her life in the ICU.

Max was alive and so was she. Melissa was getting the best possible care to enable her to recover from her injuries. Beau was safe within the veterinary hospital. Maybe she didn't completely understand the Lord's plan for her, but she needed to count her blessings.

Material things could be replaced.

People couldn't.

Calmer now, she glanced at Max, his facial expression drawn into deep lines as he stared straight ahead, watching the officers in the front seat.

Never once through this long night had he so much as hinted at growing tired of being with her. Instead, she had the impression that he was almost as worried about her well-being as he was about his sister's.

She looked away, fearing she was reading far too much into his kindness. Ted had once been as strong as Max. Not as military savvy, but Ted had been a good man, too. He was a carpenter, running his own home improvement business, slowly gaining a decent clientele and somewhat steady work until he'd been diagnosed with pancreatic cancer.

They'd had health insurance through her social worker job, but without his income and no life insurance, the bills had quickly swelled to the point she'd had to refinance their mortgage to make ends meet.

And then, when she'd known the end was near, she'd taken a leave of absence from work in order to provide palliative care for Ted at home.

He'd died in her arms on the eve of their first anniversary.

She'd wanted to die, too.

But God had other plans for her, not that she'd fully understood them. She still didn't. Overwhelmed with grief and sorrow, she'd found it difficult to seek solace in prayer. But tonight her faith in God had been restored. He must have sent Max to keep her safe.

So what if her house was gone and her precious photographs destroyed? She'd always hold her memories of Ted deep in her heart.

And she needed to be strong, to help carry out God's mission of continuing to help others, like Melissa. She certainly owed Max the return favor, after everything he'd done for her.

"Where do you want to be dropped off?" Officer Anderson asked, breaking the silence.

"At the front entrance," Max instructed.

She didn't argue, understanding Max wanted to walk to the hotel from the hospital. When Officer Schimberg opened her door, she let go of Max's hand and forced herself to get out of the car under her own power.

"Thank you," she murmured.

Officer Schimberg gave her a polite nod. She turned and waited for Max, who'd pulled their bags out of the police car, as if he'd instinctively hung on to them as a result of his military training.

"Come on," he said, taking her hand in his.

She liked the feel of his hand on hers—a little too much. They stood, waiting for the police to drive away, before he tugged on her hand.

"This way."

She followed the way he indicated, realizing he was drawing her away from the bright lights of the front entrance, around to the side of the hospital where they could blend into the darkness next to the building. It had to be close to four in the morning, but there was no sign of dawn breaking over the horizon yet.

He stopped, and she bumped into him, squashing her nose against his muscled arm. After several seconds that seemed like an eternity, he began walking again, finding the nearest sidewalk and finally leaving the relative safety of the hospital building to move toward the street.

There were several hotels on the highway. At this point, she didn't even care which one he chose. She stumbled a bit, catching herself before he decided to carry her. Again.

When they entered the hotel lobby, they must have looked like a pathetic pair with their disheveled smoke-tinged clothes and drawn faces. The lights were painfully bright, and she squinted at the young man reading a chemistry textbook behind the desk.

"We'd like two connecting rooms please," Max said, dropping their bags to the floor so he could pull out his wallet.

When she reached for her purse, he put a hand over hers, stopping her.

"No, I'll put the rooms on my credit card."

She was tired and she was thirsty, and as much as she knew she owed Max her life, she was getting mad. "Absolutely not. I insist on paying for my own room."

The muscles around his mouth tightened, and she watched in fascination, sensing he was reining in his own patience. "That's not an option. I don't want your name in any way associated with your room. Do you understand?"

Of course she understood—now that he'd explained. Feeling like a fool, she realized he was once again only trying to keep her safe. Being on the run like this, hiding from someone who wanted to hurt her, didn't come naturally. At least, not the way it seemed to for him.

Max was a soldier. She needed to listen to his wisdom.

She dropped her purse with a sigh. There was no reason to worry. As soon as she could find an ATM, she could pay him back with cash. "Yes. Sorry."

He slid the credit card over to the college student. "Two connecting rooms," he repeated.

The kid eyed them warily. "Is the second floor okay?"

"Perfect."

Five minutes later, they'd climbed the staircase to the second floor and found their rooms. Max tucked one key in his pocket and held the other in his hand as they paused outside the second door, located farther down the hall.

She swallowed hard, biting back the pathetic wish he wouldn't leave her alone.

He must have sensed her hesitation, because he unlocked her door and then paused, holding it ajar as he stared down at her.

Close. He was so close she could breathe in the comforting smell of him, could see each individual eyelash framing his kind eyes. Their gazes clashed, tension shimmering, and she held her breath, thinking he might kiss her.

But instead, he handed her the room key and took a step back. She had to catch the door with her hand before it closed.

"My room is right next door," he said, his voice low and gruff. "If you need anything, just bang on the connecting door and holler. I'll hear you."

She nodded, because that was what he expected her to do. He was being kind, a friend to someone in need. She should be grateful he wasn't making things difficult for her. "Thanks."

"Good night, Tara." He didn't smile but stood waiting patiently for her to go inside the room.

"Good night, Max." She took her overnight bag, flipped on the light inside the room and then closed the door behind her. The connecting door was immediately to her right. She moved closer, listening as he unlocked the door and entered his room.

For a moment she put her hand flat against the door jumping back in surprise when she heard a loud click as he opened the door on the other side.

"Tara?" he called.

She cleared her throat. "Yes?"

"I'm right here. All you have to do is open your door if you need anything."

"Okay." It was easy to imagine him standing on the other side. "Thank you."

"You're welcome. Get some sleep."

Silence surrounded her, intensifying the stark feeling of being alone.

She turned away. She wasn't alone, not really. God was always with her. Max was on the other side of the door. She took a few minutes to pull her belongings from her small overnight bag, grateful for the few items she'd packed. After washing her face and brushing her teeth she climbed into bed.

Closing her eyes, she prayed. *Dear Lord, thank You for sending Max to help me. Thank You for keeping us safe after the explosion. Please help Melissa and Beau recover quickly from their injuries. And please give me strength and courage to carry out Your will, Amen.*

Usually experiencing God's peace in prayer helped her to fall asleep. But not tonight. Her mind replayed those brief moments with Max standing outside her door. What was wrong with her? Had she really wanted him to kiss her? She shouldn't. She'd loved her husband.

Surely God had sent Max to keep her safe, not to replace Ted in her life. With her eyes tightly shut, she tried to center her thoughts on Ted. But his familiar features grew increasingly blurry, seeming to slide away like water swirling through her fingers, no matter how much she tried to hold fast.

Then without warning, the hazy features cleared. Her heart raced until she realized the face smiling brightly down at her wasn't Ted's.

It belonged to Max.

FIVE

Max awoke with a rush, sitting bolt upright in bed, his heart ricocheting off his ribs as he fought the crippling remnants of another flashback.

He sat for a moment, willing his heart rate to return to normal. The first flashback was to be expected. The sound of the explosion had catapulted him right back to Iraq. But dreams turning into flashbacks were a little unusual, at least for him.

Maybe the stress had brought it on. He'd spent a good hour sitting in a chair right next to the connecting door to Tara's room, unable to relax. Glancing at his watch, he realized he'd only slept for about three hours.

Not enough rest, but there was nothing to do now but to get up. He wondered how Tara was doing before abruptly realizing he should be more concerned with Lissa's progress.

A quick shower helped push the flashback deep into a crevasse of his mind, clearing away some of the fatigue. He bypassed the army gear in favor of a comfortable pair of blue jeans and a wrinkled shirt he'd found in the bottom of his duffel. As soon as he'd finished getting dressed, he used his cell phone to call the hospital.

The nurse reassured him that Lissa's condition was unchanged but stable. He thanked her and hung up. Then he called the police officer whose name the nurse had given him. A guy named James Newton answered the phone.

Max explained he was Melissa's brother, but the cop sounded impatient, like he was in a hurry. Basically, he asked for information on Gary, which Max didn't have. When Max hung up a few minutes later, he wasn't convinced the police were giving Lissa's case top priority. Newton had pretty much admitted he was planning to wait for Lissa to wake up before he went any further.

Max would have to take on the burden of finding Gary himself.

Hungry again, he considered running down to the small dining room for breakfast but thought he should wait for Tara, considering she didn't have money to spare.

A guy didn't make a lot of money in the army, but he didn't need to spend much, either. Just about everything was taken care of for him or available at steeply discounted prices.

He didn't mind giving Tara a helping hand.

It was too early to call her, barely nine in the morning, so he tried to be patient. He stood at the window, gazing at the city street outside the hotel, amazed at how busy it was even on a Saturday morning.

The ringing of his cell phone shattered the silence, startling him. The number wasn't familiar, so he answered hesitantly. "Hello?"

"Lieutenant Forrester? This is Detective Graham, with the St. Louis P.D. I took over the Carmichael case from Anderson and Schimberg. I need to talk to Ms. Carmichael about her car and her house."

Max spun away from the window and walked toward the desk. "If you give me your direct number, I'll have her call you."

Detective Graham gave him his number. "Please have her call me as soon as possible."

His fingers tightened on the receiver. "Did you find something?"

There was a pause on the other end of the line. "I understand from the officers who arrived on the scene that you've taken the role of protecting Ms. Carmichael, but even so, I'd rather talk to her about this directly."

He wanted to argue. The fact that he'd just arrived on a plane from Germany yesterday evening had ruled him out as a suspect. But Tara was an adult, and he understood the police were only following procedure. "I'll have her call you back."

He could knock on the door, but that seemed a little too personal. Using the hotel line, he dialed Tara's room, listening to the ringing on the other side of their connecting door. The phone rang several times, before going to a hotel message service. He hung up, trying not to panic.

It was still early. She could be sound asleep or in the shower. He paced the length of the cramped hotel room, waiting a full five minutes before walking over to the connecting door. His side was open—hers wasn't.

He rapped on it. "Tara? Are you awake?"

No response.

Pressing his ear to the door, he strained to listen. There was nothing but silence. He rapped again, harder. "Tara? It's Max. Open up."

Still nothing.

He grabbed the slip of paper with Detective Graham's number and his room key. He headed down to the lobby. The kid from the middle of the night was gone, and in his place was a thin, middle-aged woman with a bad bleach-blond dye job. "May I help you?"

"I need a new key for room 211."

"Your name?"

"Max Forrester." He pulled out his wallet and showed her his ID.

She entered his name into the computer. "Yes, I see you have two rooms under your name. Do you need keys for both rooms?"

"No, just 211." A stab of guilt sliced deep. He didn't have any right to invade Tara's privacy like this. If she was sound asleep in her bed, then he was going to feel like a jerk for disturbing her.

But if she wasn't...

Steeling his resolve, he took the newly programmed

key card and rushed back upstairs to the second floor. Outside her door, he hesitated only for a moment before swiftly unlocking the door.

Holding his breath, he pushed the door open as quietly as possible, so as not to wake her.

The bed was empty. Through the open bathroom door he saw that it too was empty.

Panic surged, choking him. Where could she have gone? There were at least four hotels all within walking distance of the hospital. How could her stalker have known where they were staying? Had the guy somehow managed to follow them after all?

His gaze swept the room, absorbing every detail. Her overnight bag was still there, but he didn't see her cell phone or her purse—the small, black one she'd checked at the bus stop when she'd looked for money.

Get a grip, he told himself. If her stalker had found her, she probably wouldn't have had time to take her purse. The room was neat and tidy, no evidence of a struggle. He would have heard an intruder through the connecting door. Tara was a fighter; she wouldn't have gone easily.

Taking one deep breath after another, he calmed his racing thoughts. Tara didn't have a car. She couldn't have gone far. He couldn't call her, because he hadn't taken the time to program her number into his phone.

He left her room, shutting the door behind him. He followed the bacon smell to the dining room, but Tara wasn't among the small smattering of guests enjoying their breakfast.

Where else could she be? The hospital? He left the

hotel, jogged across the street and crossed the hospital campus. The hotel he'd chosen was way on the back side of the hospital, as far from the front entrance as possible.

This time the doors were open. He didn't stop at the information desk but headed directly up to the ICU.

He had to call in from the hallway phone and give his name to the woman inside seated at the desk.

"Come on in," the ward clerk responded, unlocking the doors.

He walked to room eight, looking first at Lissa, who appeared to be resting comfortably as the nurse promised, before noticing Tara, who was seated in a chair beside Melissa's bed. Her head was bowed over her clasped hands. She was praying.

Tara was safe.

Now that he'd found her, he stood uncertainly, not wanting to disturb her. Her praying made him uncomfortable, even though it reminded him of his life before the army, when he'd once had faith in God. Before his best friend, Keith, had died. Before he'd lost his faith. Her peaceful presence drew him forward, until he remembered how God had seemingly abandoned his soldiers, especially Keith. The memory of his best friend, dying too young, held him back.

Tara was a believer. He wasn't. Not anymore.

She was also a young, grieving widow. An enticing mix of fragility and strength, stubbornness and beauty. It would be too easy to lower his defenses, allowing himself to be drawn to her.

He took one step back and then another until he was

in the hallway, out of sight. The best thing he could do for Tara was to leave her alone.

She'd found peace. A peace he envied.

A peace far beyond his reach.

Tara bowed her head and prayed for strength. Prayed for wisdom in following the correct path her Lord had chosen. For courage to do what He asked of her. She also prayed for Melissa's swift recovery. She stayed at Melissa's bedside for over an hour and finally found the serenity of God's presence.

She lifted her head and gazed at Melissa. Looking past the cuts and bruises, the endotracheal tube sticking out of her mouth connected to the ventilator and the heart monitor beeping above her head, she might have been sleeping. Resting. Hopefully gathering her strength to heal in spite of the seriousness of her injuries.

She wasn't afraid of Gary finding Melissa anymore, considering the nurses planned to put Melissa under an alias once Max arrived.

They needed to find Gary. And the stalker.

They? Wait a minute. Why had her mind already linked her and Max together as a team? Max needed to find Gary. She needed to find her stalker. Max had already helped her enough.

No wonder she couldn't clearly visualize Ted's face anymore. She was spending too much time with Max.

A wave of guilt hit hard. Was it wrong of her to enjoy her time with Max? He was only a friend, but she still felt as if she were somehow being unfaithful to her memories of Ted.

She'd never love anyone the way she loved Ted. So there was nothing for her to feel guilty about. Now, if only she could make herself believe it.

The police wanted a list of potential clients who might carry a grudge against her, so she'd give it to them. Keeping busy would only help. She quickly stood. Assaulted by dizziness, she swayed, grabbing onto Melissa's bed rail for support and blinking back the darkness. Lack of food. Lack of sleep. She might be able to fix the former if she could get access to an ATM.

Sleep was impossible.

She waited for the light-headedness to pass. She needed to get back to the hotel before Max discovered she was missing. Glancing down at Melissa, she took her client's hand in hers and leaned close.

"Fight to get better, Melissa. Max needs you. He's only here for a couple of weeks. Please get better so you can talk to him before his leave is up." The thought of Max heading back to Iraq, without knowing his sister's fate, made her heart ache for him. "God is with you. If you trust in Him, he'll keep you safe. I'll be back to see you soon. Take care, Melissa." She gently squeezed Melissa's hand before letting go.

With coma patients, hearing was often the last sense to go and the first to recover. And God created miracles every day. She hoped at least the essence of her words had gotten through. She wondered if Melissa would respond better to Max's deep voice.

She left Melissa's room and walked down the hall, surprised to find Max near the nurse's station talking to one of the doctors. She quickened her step so that she could hear what the doctor was saying.

Max acknowledged her arrival with a curt nod. She sensed he wasn't happy with her.

"We need to do another CT scan of her head," the doctor was saying, "to make sure the bleeding and subsequent swelling of her brain hasn't gotten worse. If it hasn't, then we believe she should recover without too much residual damage."

And if it had gotten worse? She didn't voice the question, because the implication was clear. If there was more bleeding or swelling, her chances of recovering were slim.

"So there is a chance she'll wake up?" Max asked.

The doctor nodded. "Certainly. There's a good chance she'll wake up. Head injuries can be tricky though. We need to watch the brain very carefully. Right now we're keeping her sedated, so that the swelling has a chance to go down, giving her a chance to recover."

"Thank you," Max said, offering his hand.

The doctor shook it. "You're welcome. We'll be in touch if her condition changes."

Max turned to her as the doctor walked away. "You took several years off my life disappearing like that without a word," he said in a low, accusatory tone. "I looked everywhere for you."

"I'm sorry," she said, truly feeling bad. Deep grooves of exhaustion creased his face, and his mouth was drawn in a tight line. "I couldn't sleep. I thought I'd be back before you even knew I was gone. Maybe I should have woken you up, but that didn't seem fair. There was no reason for both of us to be awake."

"Fair?" Max let out a loud snort. "Worrying me to death wasn't fair, either. I would have rather gone without sleep. But when I was trying to find you, I realized I didn't have your cell-phone number." Max pulled his phone from his pocket. "We're going to fix that right now."

"I'm sorry," one of the nurses interrupted with a polite smile, "but you can't use your cell phone in here."

She didn't think his expression could get any more grim, but it did. "Fine," he muttered between clenched teeth. "Come on, let's get some breakfast."

"I need to go down to the lobby first to get money from the ATM," she said, following him out of the ICU.

He glanced down at her as they headed for the elevators. "We'll have time for that later. Do you mind if we eat first?"

She supposed she owed him one for sneaking out on him. She didn't want to admit she'd left the hotel because she'd been thinking too much about Max. "I don't mind."

"Thanks."

The elevator ride down to the cafeteria was silent. He gestured for her to precede him in the cafeteria line.

She wasn't very hungry but the fluffy Belgian waffles drew her gaze, looking the most appetizing of the selections so she took a small helping topped with fresh strawberries. Max went for the more traditional hearty fare of bacon and eggs. As he paid for their meals, she mentally tallied up what she owed him, vowing to make good on her debts.

After spending the past eighteen months pulling herself out from beneath a mountain of bills, she wasn't about to head down that slippery slope again.

She silently thanked God for the food He'd provided before picking up her fork. When she was finished, she noticed Max staring at her curiously, but he didn't say anything. He shoved a forkful of eggs in his mouth.

He didn't swear or make inappropriate comments, but that only meant he'd been raised by someone who'd drilled good manners into his head, not that he'd been brought up Christian.

The idea that he might not believe in God distressed her.

Max ate with a single-minded determination, as if he were afraid someone might yank the food out from under his nose. She ate slowly, savoring every bite.

He didn't talk, not until he'd finished his food. And then, he was all business. "What is your cell-phone number?"

She gave him the number and watched as he entered it into his phone. He reached out his hand. "Now yours."

Growing a little annoyed with his attitude, she simply picked up her phone and raised a brow. "I can do it."

He sighed and then gave his number so she could program her own phone.

"Thanks," she said, closing her phone. "Are you always this bossy?"

He stared at her for a long minute. "Yes, I guess I am. Comes with being a platoon leader, I imagine."

She immediately felt ashamed of her annoyance. Of course he would be used to giving orders. "You need to remember you're not responsible for me, the way you are for your men," she said softly.

He stared at her for a long moment. "Point taken. The reason I was looking for you earlier was to let you know Detective Graham called. He wants to talk to you."

"Graham? What happened to Officer Anderson?"

"Apparently Detective Graham has taken over the case. Here's his number." Max slid a crumpled scrap of paper across the cafeteria table toward her. "He wouldn't talk to me, only to you."

Her mouth went dry as she stared at Max's bold scrawl. She slowly reopened her phone and punched in the numbers. She held her breath as she waited for the detective to answer.

"Graham."

"This is Tara Carmichael. Max told me you called?"

"Yes. Ms. Carmichael, we're finished with your car, and I'm sorry to say, we didn't find any usable fingerprints."

"No fingerprints?" She was disappointed. If the police had found fingerprints, they would have had a chance at finding her stalker since many of her clients had their prints on file.

"No. And we're still investigating the cause of your house explosion, but you need to know that the damage is pretty bad. You need to give your insurance company a call."

She closed her eyes, her head throbbing painfully as the lack of sleep caught up with her. She had insurance to cover the damage, but there was also a deductible to pay. And her house was already heavily mortgaged.

"Ms. Carmichael? Are you still there?"

She opened her eyes, pushing the worry aside, knowing she needed to leave her future in God's hands. She was conscious of Max's gaze on her. "Yes. I'm still here."

"The arson investigator is on-site, and he's requesting you come out to speak with him. The heat of the fire has abated enough for him to investigate the source of the blaze. I'm following up on some other leads, so I won't be out there for a while. Can you make it?"

"Of course I'll be there." She snapped her phone shut.

Max was already stacking their dirty dishes together onto one tray. "I'll rent a car. After that, we'll head over."

She wanted to tell him no, that she'd go to meet the arson investigator by herself, but she couldn't do it. Just the thought of seeing the wreckage of her house was enough to make her stomach churn. She knew she shouldn't care about material things, but the house was the home she'd shared with Ted. "The police have released my car. All I need to do is to call a garage to have new tires put on. Should only take a day or two and then we can return your rental car."

He frowned. "Not a good plan. This guy knows your car, considering he slashed all four tires. A rental is much safer."

Unable to argue, she followed as he carried their tray of dishes to the conveyor belt located near the cafeteria exit.

The amount of debt she owed him just kept adding up. "First stop, the lobby."

He gave a resigned sigh. "All right."

She tried to withdraw money from the machine, but it wouldn't give her any. The message read, "Insufficient funds."

"That can't be right," she muttered, trying again. The ache in her stomach intensified. She knew she didn't have a lot of money in her checking account, but how could the total have gone that low?

"Is there a problem?" Max asked.

She hesitated, and then shook her head. "Not really, the machine isn't working right. I'll stop by my bank on Monday."

"All right. Let's get that rental car."

The rental process took longer than planned. A few hours later, Max finally drove to her house so they could meet with the arson investigator. On the way, she kept thinking about that ATM message. She didn't want to panic over nothing, but it was odd that the amount was so low. Had there been some large check she'd written that she didn't remember? Her mortgage payments were automatic. Maybe there'd been a mistake where twice the amount had come out of her account instead of the normal payment.

When they arrived at her house, and climbed from the car, her worries over her checking account faded with her first glimpse of the charred wreckage. Max took her hand in his.

There wasn't much left of her house. And the parts that were left were likely severely water damaged from the firefighters battling the blaze.

Max's hand on hers tightened. "Are you all right?"

Not really, she thought, but she forced herself to nod. This was all a part of God's plan. She needed to stay strong. She took several steps toward her house. The arson investigator, an older man with dark hair, liberally sprinkled with various shades of gray, caught sight of them and came forward.

"Ms. Carmichael?" he asked.

"Yes." Her voice was embarrassingly weak, so she forced herself to stop acting like a wimp. She lifted her chin. "I'm Tara Carmichael, and this is Max Forrester."

"Fire Captain Hank Meyers." He introduced himself. "I'm serving as the arson investigator on this case. We found the source of the explosion. There was a small bomb with a crude timer planted in the ceiling rafters of your basement, directly beneath your bedroom."

"I'm not surprised," Max said grimly.

A bomb. With a timer. Ticking away, long into the

night, waiting to explode. Seeing the extensive damage in the harsh light of day, she humbly appreciated just how close she'd come to dying.

The entire event was just as Max and Officer Anderson had suspected. If she hadn't left with Max last night, caving to his controlling attitude, she would never have known what hit her. Her hands began to shake. She tightly clasped them together.

Who had done this? And why? Who could possibly hate her enough to painstakingly and coldheartedly plan to kill her?

She looked away from the house, unable to bear looking at the destruction anymore. A brown car rolled slowly down the street. She barely noticed at first, but then she caught sight of the driver.

A man wearing a navy blue baseball cap pulled low over his eyes.

It took a split second for the significance to sink in.

She grabbed Max's arm and gave it a hard shake. "There! That's the guy who's been following me!"

SIX

"Where?" Max spun around and gave her a slight push to keep her protected behind his body. His fierce gaze raked the area. "I don't see him."

"Driving that brown car." She stepped to the side. She pointed to the vehicle, which now drove quickly down the street toward the intersection. She stared after it intently. "I can't see the license plate. It's full of dirt. Maybe KNP for the first part?"

The car careened around the corner, its back end fishtailing before it disappeared from view.

"Did you see him, too?" she demanded, looking at Captain Meyers.

The older man nodded. "I saw him. Didn't get a good look at the tag, though."

Max had his phone in his hand. "Graham? Tara's stalker is headed east on Parker Road, toward Jamison. He's in a brown Ford Taurus. License plate starts with KNP. Will you send your closest squad?" He listened for a moment before snapping his phone shut.

"They're on it," he said.

"Do you think they'll catch him?" She relaxed a bit now that the police had been notified.

"I hope so." Max put an arm around her, giving her a gentle, reassuring squeeze. "I really hope so."

"So do I." She took a deep breath, inhaling Max's scent, feeling safe beside him. She was grateful he was there with her, although she knew she was becoming too dependent on him. Hadn't this very dilemma caused her to lose sleep last night?

She forced herself to break away from his comforting embrace. The move stung sharply as if she'd ripped a bandage off her arm. "I need to go to my office."

Max stared at her like she'd sprouted purple hair and declared she could fly. "What?"

"I need to go to my office." She kept her tone matter-of-fact, but she wasn't in the mood to argue. She was tired of being a victim, of feeling as if she were at the stalker's mercy. Had he driven by her house this morning to gloat over the destruction he'd left behind? The thought made her shudder. She needed to take action. Doing something constructive would help. Wallowing in self-pity would not.

God helps those who use His strength to help themselves.

Resolutely turning her back on the burned mass that was once her home, she faced Max. She should also follow the detective's advice and call the insurance company, especially since her house was likely a total loss.

"To review my case files," she added, when Max still

looked confused. "So I can make a list of people associated with my clients who might have a grudge against me."

The sooner they found this guy, the sooner she could get on with rebuilding her life. Her home. And the safer she'd feel. Maybe the police would catch the guy in the brown Ford Taurus. They were already checking into Tyrone Adams. She almost hoped the man stalking her was someone associated with one of her clients.

Because that would mean they had a good chance of finding him, soon.

"No. Absolutely not," Max countered in a firm tone. "He's already shown up here at your house. The next obvious place to find you would be your office. He knows where it is. He vandalized your car while you were working. Let's go back to the hotel and give the police time to do their job."

She understood his reluctance, but she didn't want to go back to the hotel. Sitting alone in her hotel room held little appeal. "Max, it's Saturday. There's no reason for him to think I'd go to work on the weekend when I never have before." She'd always used her Saturday mornings to work from home. Short of a drastic emergency, she'd never gone into the office. "He's already seen us here, I'm sure my reaction was exactly what he was looking for."

"I don't like it," he muttered, half under his breath.

The resigned expression in his eyes convinced her she'd hit upon the one argument that might sway him.

"I have to do this," she said in a low, urgent tone.

"Don't you understand? I need to do whatever it takes to help put this man behind bars before he hurts someone." As far as she knew, she'd been his only target. But what if that changed?

"All right. We'll go to your office, *after* we stop by the restaurant where Lissa worked." His tone was a bit testy. "I need to talk to some of the people she worked with—there's a chance one of them knows Gary or has at least seen the guy."

She winced, not liking how her problems were once again drawing Max away from finding the man who'd hurt Melissa. She shouldn't stand in his way—her problems weren't his. Chagrined, she nodded. "You're right. The restaurant is closer anyway."

"And we need to eat," Max added, relaxing now that she'd agreed to his plan.

She was about to protest but then realized she was hungry after all. The Belgian waffles she'd eaten for breakfast seemed like a long time ago. Normally she didn't have much of an appetite. Surely this new change was related to stressing about the identity of her stalker, rather than being with Max.

Shaking off her thoughts, she turned toward the fire captain, who stood a few feet away, finishing up a phone call. Had he reported the guy in the Taurus, too? "Excuse me, Captain," she said when he finished. "But is there anything else you need from us?"

"Just the name of your insurance company, Ms. Carmichael." He glanced at her with kind eyes, taking a small notebook out of his breast pocket. "I'll need to report this as arson. But given your circumstances and the ongoing police investigation, I doubt anyone will suspect you of setting the bomb yourself."

Her brows shot up in surprise. "I would hope not. Why would I destroy the only place I have to live?" She dug through her purse and handed over her insurance card.

Captain Meyers jotted down the information.

"Are you ready?" Max had taken a hold of her arm again. She liked the warmth of his hand on her skin a little too much. With a pang of regret, she subtly pulled away.

"Yes."

As they walked toward his rental car, he sent her a quizzical glance. She avoided his gaze and kept silent on the short trip from her house to the family restaurant where Melissa worked. The night they'd walked home after sharing dinner seemed like days ago, instead of not even twenty-four hours.

"Hello," the hostess greeted them with a friendly smile. "Table for two?" she asked.

"My name is Max Forrester. Do you know my sister, Melissa? She works here as a server."

"Sure, I know Melissa. She was supposed to work today but hasn't come in yet."

"She's in the hospital in the ICU. I should have told you sooner. Please let the manager know, will you? I'll bring in documentation from the doctor if needed."

"In the ICU?" the woman's eyes widened in alarm. "I'm sorry to hear that. I hope she's getting better?"

"The doctor tells me she's serious but stable.

Actually, I'd like to talk to a few of Melissa's friends. Anyone who might be working today."

The server frowned a bit, as if she were hesitant to give out too much information. "Annie knows Melissa fairly well, but I'm afraid she's pretty busy. This is our lunchtime rush."

"I understand," Max replied, flashing an easy smile. "Would you mind seating us in her section? We can wait a few minutes for a table to open up if necessary."

The woman scanned her seating chart. "I think I can squeeze you into Annie's section." She picked up two menus. "Follow me, please."

Tara gave Max credit, obviously he assumed they'd get more cooperation from the servers if they ordered a meal.

"Here you go." The hostess showed them to a small table tucked into the back corner of the restaurant.

"This is great, thanks." Max chose the side of the booth where he could see the entire restaurant. Tara slid in across from him.

Annie was a young girl in her early twenties with bright burgundy streaks in her brown hair. She took their order and then hurried away before Max could ask his questions.

"Didn't you want to talk to her?" Tara asked in a low tone.

"I will, don't worry."

When Annie returned with their drinks, Max stopped her before she could leave. "Annie, I'm Max Forrester, Melissa's brother. Do you have a minute to talk?"

Annie's eyes turned wary. "I'm pretty busy."

"Please?" Max persisted. "Melissa's been hurt. She's in the ICU at St. Louis General."

Annie gasped. "In the ICU? No wonder she didn't come in for work today. What happened?"

Max hesitated, glancing at Tara, clearly unsure how much to reveal. "We think her boyfriend, Gary, hurt her. She has cracked ribs and a head injury."

"Oh, no. Poor Melissa," Annie murmured, her expression troubled.

"Do you know Gary? Have you seen him? Can you describe him for me?" Max asked.

The young waitress slowly shook her head. "I saw him once but only from a distance. I didn't really pay attention. He was tall, sort of like you, with short reddish-brown hair." She shrugged her shoulders helplessly. "I didn't get a close look at him, but he was frowning, as if he were mad about something."

Max leaned forward, anxiously. "Can you think of anyone who might remember him more clearly? Someone who knows his last name?"

"Not off the top of my head," Annie admitted. "Melissa was great to work with, but she didn't socialize much with the people here. I got the impression she was always looking for something better. She liked hanging out with people who had money."

Tara frowned, not liking the sound of that. She'd often wondered why Melissa kept going back with Gary. Could money have something to do with it?

"All right," Max said in a dejected tone. "But if you

think of anything that can help us, please call me. Here's my number." He slid a piece of paper toward her.

"Sure." Annie took the note, giving him a hesitant smile. "I'll be back when your lunch orders are up."

When Annie left, Max turned toward Tara. "I was hoping for something more substantial."

"I know." She longed to reach out to comfort him. "At least we know he's tall with short reddish-brown hair. That's more than what we had a few hours ago."

"But it's not enough to take to the police." Max took a gulp of his lemonade.

"Have you spoken to the officer assigned to Melissa's case?" she asked.

"James Newton. Yeah, but I don't think he's doing much at this point other than waiting for Lissa to wake up, so he can question her about Gary. He told me Lissa's neighbors heard the fight and called the police. When the officers arrived, her apartment door was open and Lissa was lying on the floor unconscious. There was no sign of Gary, only an elderly woman rendering aid to Lissa. Her eyesight is poor, and she couldn't give a useful description of Gary." He scowled. "They're not giving Lissa's case high priority."

Possibly because Melissa hadn't pressed charges the last time, Tara realized. "That's not fair, what if she doesn't wake up?" The minute the words were out of her mouth she wanted to snatch them back. She hadn't meant to insinuate that his sister wouldn't survive her injuries.

"Then he'll treat it as a homicide," Max said grimly.

"I'm sorry," Tara said, covering his hand with hers. "Don't worry. Melissa will be fine."

"I hope so." He stared down at their clasped hands for a moment and then gave a gentle squeeze. "Thanks. Having you here makes this much easier."

His sincere gratitude made her blush. She was happy to help, but she didn't like being a financial drain on him, either. Sitting here at lunch reminded her of their dinner the night before. And their breakfast earlier that morning. She wanted to offer to pay for their meal, but she didn't have enough money with her. And according to the ATM, she didn't have any left in her checking account.

She could offer her credit card, but she might reach her limit fairly quickly. She was still making hefty payments, trying to bring the balance down from when Ted was so ill.

What if the missing money wasn't just a bank error? "Max, there's something you need to know," she began but was interrupted by Annie's return.

"Here you go," Annie declared, setting a large tray down beside them. "You know, I was thinking about what you said, and I'm pretty sure Melissa had a picture of Gary on her cell phone."

"She did?" Max leaned forward. "Are you sure?"

Annie nodded. "I remember because she claimed Gary was camera shy, always refusing to have his picture taken, but that she'd gotten one of him without his knowing."

How odd. Tara exchanged a glance with Max. Why wouldn't Gary want his picture taken? Max looked just as perplexed. He smiled. "Thanks, Annie. You've been a great help."

"No problem." She put her hand on her hip and glanced over their meals. "Is there anything else I can get you?"

"No, we should be fine," Max assured her.

"All right. I'll be back in a bit to check on things." She spun away.

"Where do you think her cell phone could be?" Max muttered.

"We can check her apartment," Tara suggested. She gave a quick, silent prayer of thanks to the Lord for providing her food before taking a bite of her salad.

"I don't have a key," Max said, between bites of his steak sandwich. "And I don't think her apartment manager is going to let me in."

"We could check the hospital," Tara said helpfully. "If she had any valuables, like a purse or a cell phone when she was admitted, the hospital security department would lock them up for her."

"Unless the police took them," Max pointed out.

"But why would they? Melissa's just a case of domestic abuse, and they know her boyfriend was involved. You said yourself they weren't actively looking for Gary."

"True. All we need is her cell phone." Max's eyes were full of hope. "We're finally making progress."

"Absolutely."

They finished their meal in silence. Annie returned, clearing away their dirty dishes. "Anything else? Did you save room for dessert?"

"No, thanks," Max said.

"I'll leave your bill here, then." Annie left the slip of paper facedown on the table. "Oh, and if you're still looking for information on Gary, you might try getting in touch with Peggy Sue Hamilton."

"Peggy Sue Hamilton?" Max echoed. "Is she another server?"

"She used to be," Annie leaned forward, dropping her voice to a whisper. "She was fired last week for being a no call, no-show. But she and Melissa used to go out sometimes. Peggy Sue might know more about Gary."

"Do you have her number?" Max asked.

"Sure. I jotted it down for you." She handed a slip of paper over to Max. Tara noticed the young waitress seemed rather impressed with Max, going out of her way to help him. And Tara was dismayed to realize she didn't appreciate the way the younger woman smiled so engagingly at him.

"Thanks again, Annie. You've been very helpful." Max didn't seem to notice the young woman's bright, pretty smile.

"Any time. Please come back to let me know how Melissa is doing."

"Sure." Max glanced at the bill and took out his wallet to count out the correct amount, including a substantial tip.

Tara couldn't blame him. After all, Annie had given them a lot of great information. At least now they had a place to start in their search for Gary.

They walked out to the car and climbed inside. Once they were seated, Max's cell phone rang.

"It's the detective," he said, opening his phone. "Did you get him?" When his expression tightened and his mouth thinned, Tara knew Detective Graham wasn't providing good news. "All right, let us know if you get anything from the car. Thanks for calling."

She met Max's gaze as he shut his phone. "He got away, didn't he?"

"Yeah. The brown Ford Taurus was stolen. Your stalker abandoned it about ten miles from your house and must have taken off on foot or stolen another car. The police are going to check the car for fingerprints, but if they don't find any, we're right back where we started."

Max leaned against the wall of Tara's cramped office, trying to give her as much room as possible. Her forehead was scrunched with intense concentration as she riffled through her paper files, jotting names on a sheet of paper.

When she'd insisted on stopping at her office, he couldn't say no. Especially not after Graham had let him know her stalker had gotten away.

Tara continued to work, her attention centered on the task in front of her. He shifted, looking away.

He was too aware of her. Every move. Every emotion flitting across her features. At lunch he'd told her how much he appreciated her being there with him.

It was true.

He was startled by how much he was already starting to care for her.

He needed to get a grip. This was a mistake he'd made before. In Iraq, there was a nurse, Clare, who'd worked in the triage hospital they'd set up in Baghdad. She'd come to him for help when one of the men she'd dated, a guy in his platoon, had been unable to accept it when she'd told him their relationship was over. He'd offered her protection, and a shoulder to cry on. During those weeks he'd helped her out, they'd grown closer. As the weeks passed and they'd spent even more time together, he'd believed he was starting to fall in love with her.

But his feelings hadn't been reciprocated.

Clare told him he was a good friend—and that she'd appreciated his help—but that she'd fallen in love with someone else, a doctor who'd also worked in the triage area.

He'd felt like a fool, having mistaken her gratitude for something more.

His bruised heart hadn't been Clare's fault. He couldn't resist helping out a woman in trouble. Hadn't he proven that again with Tara?

He didn't mind providing a helping hand, but he needed to learn how to do that without getting emotionally involved.

"That's it," Tara said finally, sitting back in her chair with a sigh. "I have a list of every man who was involved in any of my cases who even roughly fits the description of my stalker."

He straightened and pushed away from the wall. "How many?"

"Twenty-five." At his incredulous expression, she grimaced. "I know, it's a lot. But I went back a couple of years, just in case. I know the stalker has just come after me recently, but it's possible one of these men was in jail for a while and may have been recently released on parole. I didn't want to take the chance of missing anyone."

"Wise move," he agreed. "Do you have a fax machine here? We could fax the list to Graham."

"Sure." When she smiled at him, his stomach clenched and he knew he was in trouble. Deep trouble. Tara was too nice. Too likable.

Too vulnerable.

She's a widow, he reminded himself sternly. She loved her husband. She had no interest in him.

Using his phone, he contacted Graham for a fax number. Once the list was safely in the hands of the police, he grew anxious to leave. They had several clues to follow up regarding Gary. He'd already called Peggy Sue's cell phone but had gotten her voice mail, so he'd left a message. And he was anxious to get Lissa's purse from the hospital.

"Are you ready to go?" he asked, opening the office door.

"I have to make one more phone call first, to check on Beau."

He waited for Tara to make the call. From the upbeat tone of her voice he could tell Beau was progressing well. When she hung up, she smiled at him. "Guess what? Beau is going to be released tomorrow."

"That's great," he said warily, wondering what they'd do with the dog once they'd picked him up. The hotel wasn't likely to allow pets, although he was willing to find a new place to stay, if it would mean making Tara happy.

She didn't seem to notice his hesitation as she quickly locked up the office. They made their way outside.

Inside his rental car he started the car and waited for a break in the traffic. He noticed Tara's smile had disappeared. Instead she was frowning intently at the list she'd created.

"Any of those seem more likely now that you've had a chance to go through the files?" he asked, as he merged into traffic.

"Yes." She frowned. "There's a man I'd forgotten about. Steve Jasper. He was extremely angry with me two years ago. I hardly remembered the incident because it happened right after the doctors told me there was nothing more we could do for my husband, Ted, who'd been diagnosed with pancreatic cancer, except make him comfortable. I took a leave of absence from work shortly afterward."

He could imagine her husband's plight had been far more important than one of her cases. "So what did happen?"

"I recommended his ten-year-old daughter be removed from his custody because the school reported suspicious bruises. He had a violent streak I didn't like—in fact, he lost his temper in the courtroom, which clinched the judge's decision."

A warning chill snaked down his spine. If that guy had laid a hand on Tara...

"What do you mean, he lost his temper? How?"

Tara swallowed hard. "He threatened to kill me."

SEVEN

Max tightened his grip on the steering wheel, her words echoing over and over in his mind. He kept his voice even with an effort. "I hope you put Jasper on the top of your list."

"I did. And I put a star by his name, asking Detective Graham to follow up on him, first." She dropped her gaze. She carefully folded her list and tucked it in her purse.

He tried to concentrate on driving, but his thoughts raced. If Steve Jasper was the guilty man, Max hoped they caught him—and soon. Arson and attempted murder were not petty crimes. The guy deserved a steep jail sentence.

His admiration for Tara grew, as he realized just how much she dealt with every day in her quest to help people. Clare, too, had given a lot to her patients, wounded soldiers from his platoon and others. He didn't want to think about the similarities between Tara and Clare. "Good. Jasper definitely sounds like he could be our guy."

"I agree." Tara sat back in her seat with a small sigh.

Having a list of suspects should help the police move forward with her case. The bombing of her house had given her case a higher priority. Now that they'd done what they could to find Tara's stalker, he wanted to concentrate on finding Gary. "Let's head to the hospital, to see if we can get Lissa's purse and cell phone."

"Sure."

During the ride to the hospital, Tara fell asleep, her head rolling a little against the back of the seat.

He pulled up to a stop in the hospital visitor parking lot. Leaving the car running, he turned to look at her. Tara looked so peaceful that he hated to wake her.

She was clearly exhausted, no doubt having gotten little to no sleep last night. He wished she'd let him drop her off at the hotel while he searched for Gary. But at the same time he knew Tara was much safer with him.

If this guy, Steve Jasper, was the one who'd bombed her house, leaving Tara to fend for herself was not an option.

After giving her another ten minutes to rest, he finally shut off the car and reached over to give her a little shake. "Tara? We're here."

"Hmm?" She turned her head toward him, her eyelashes fluttering open. When she realized she'd fallen asleep, she abruptly sat up and rubbed at her eyes. "Sorry about that."

"No problem." He climbed from the car and waited for her to walk around to join him. "I'd like to stop and visit Lissa first."

"Of course."

Tara accompanied him up to the fourth floor ICU, where he was told Lissa's condition remained serious but stable. The nurse explained that they were monitoring the pressure in her brain through a special monitor, so they could make sure the swelling wouldn't get too bad. He was grateful for the care they were giving Lissa. He tried to look on the bright side of things, knowing she hadn't gotten any worse, but it wasn't easy. His sister's bruised and swollen face haunted him.

Why had she stayed with Gary? Why hadn't she pressed charges against him? Or moved?

The little bit he was learning from Lissa's acquaintances hadn't reassured him. Had his sister really been so focused on money? If so, why? Was she finding it that hard to make ends meet?

Maybe when his tour of duty was over he needed to come home. He could support Lissa while she went back to school. Her chances of getting a better paying job increased substantially if she earned a college education.

He wasn't sure what sort of job he could get in the private sector, but he had a strong back and didn't mind hard work. He was sure he could pick up something.

After a short visit with Lissa, he turned to leave. Tara knew the hospital better than he did, so she led the way downstairs to the main security desk. Getting Lissa's belongings wasn't as easy as he'd thought. The security guard on duty wanted them to come back Monday, during normal business hours, but Tara was persistent, and in the end, the security guard finally relented.

"I'll need your signatures here and here," he said, indicating the blank lines on the bottom of two different forms. "And if my boss has an issue with this on Monday, I'm going to tell him to call you."

"That would be fine, we won't mind a phone call at all," Tara assured him. "Thanks so much for your help."

Max signed the forms and took Lissa's handbag from the security officer. He waited until they were back inside the rental car before opening it.

He stared at the jumbled contents inside before glancing at Tara. "This feels wrong," he murmured. "Going through Lissa's personal stuff like this feels wrong."

"I know." Her gaze shimmered with sympathy. "But Gary needs to be stopped. We wouldn't be doing this if there was another way to find him. I don't think Melissa will mind."

She was right, but that didn't make invading his sister's privacy any easier. Hoping to find the phone, he fished through the purse. The phone wasn't there. He found her wallet, but there was very little cash and not much else. There was a book of matches from some bar, which was very strange since he didn't think Lissa smoked. And he found her keys.

"No phone," he said finally, setting Lissa's purse aside. "But we do have her keys. Maybe the phone is in her apartment. Do you want me to drop you off at the hotel before I head out?"

"I'd rather go with you, if you don't mind."

He tucked the keys into his pocket and started the car. "Okay, but this is only going to make you a party to the crime."

"We're not breaking the law," Tara protested. "We have her keys, so we're not breaking and entering. Finding Gary and putting him behind bars is the best thing we can do for Melissa right now. Other than praying."

Max nodded, although he wasn't so sure the praying bit was really going to help. Tara's connection to God seemed to keep her grounded, but he didn't have the same spiritual ties she did.

Were her prayers strong enough to overcome his lapse? He hoped so. He wanted to believe God would listen to Tara on his sister's behalf.

At this point, Lissa needed all the help she could get.

Tara listened to Max's one-sided phone conversation and realized he was talking to Peggy Sue. She fished out a pen and paper so Max could write down Peggy Sue's address. After he hung up the phone, he looked at her, his eyes bright with satisfaction.

"Peggy Sue is willing to talk to us. She has met Gary and thinks she can give us a more detailed description of the guy. I think we'd be better off going to see her first and then searching for the phone in Lissa's apartment. She may have a couple of pictures on there."

"Sounds logical. Although remember what Annie said about him being camera shy? I doubt we'll find more than one picture."

"Yeah, I remember." Max scowled. "I don't get it. Don't you think that's strange? I mean, why would he be so camera shy?"

"I don't know, but I can't imagine the reasons are good ones." She felt a little guilty for not telling Max about Melissa's substance-abuse problem. Six months ago, Melissa had been arrested for possession of crack cocaine and in order to stay out of jail, she'd been given the option of working with Tara to get help and for follow up random drug testing. Melissa's drug problem wasn't her secret to share, but she hoped the knowledge wouldn't impact their ability to track down Gary. There were some lines she couldn't cross, and as Melissa's caseworker, divulging private information was one of those lines. "It could be he's wanted by the police."

"I already thought of that," Max admitted, navigating the St. Louis streets with ease. "And I hope he is wanted by the cops so that once we find him he'll be immediately arrested."

She had to smile at his optimism. "Works for me."

"I can't even imagine leaving here to go back to Iraq without finding him," Max said in a low tone. "We just have to find that cell-phone picture."

So much for his optimism. She reached over and put a hand on his arm. "Don't worry. God is guiding us. We'll find Gary soon. You'll see."

He didn't look at her but kept his eyes on the road. "I hope you're right."

"I am," she said firmly.

"Okay, once we get to Harwood Avenue, then I'll

need your help in searching out addresses to find Peggy Sue's."

"All right." She stared at Max's strong hands on the steering wheel, amazed at how comfortable she was with him. She felt as if she knew him better than some of her clients, which was amazing since twenty-four hours ago, she didn't even know he existed.

And now they were partners, working together to find Gary and her stalker.

She tore her gaze away, forcing herself to look out the window. It had been her idea to get Melissa's purse from hospital security, but she knew very well that she and Max weren't exactly partners. She was more of a liability than a help. He was going along with her wishes just to keep her safe.

Lieutenant Max Forrester was an honorable man. In more ways than one.

She sighed. As much as she admired Max, she was beginning to realize he could never be more than a friend. Not just because she'd loved Ted and wasn't interested in replacing him. And not just because Max was only in town for a short while, scheduled to return to Iraq in nineteen days.

But because every time she mentioned God, faith or prayer, he tensed up, looked away or changed the subject. He'd never come right out and said he didn't believe in God, but she sensed he wasn't open to the concept.

She stared down at her entwined hands. Was this part of God's plan for her? To help Max understand and believe? And if so, how would she even begin? They didn't have a lot of spare time on their hands; in fact they'd hardly had time to eat and sleep.

Max was under pressure to find Gary, which was very understandable. And she wanted to help. Yet she couldn't ignore God's mission, either.

"Here's the Harwood apartment complex," Max said, breaking into her thoughts. "Help me find the 400 building."

She peered out the window. "There, the even numbered buildings are on the right. Second one down should be the 400 building."

"I see it." Max pulled into a vacant parking space marked for visitors, looking around with frank admiration. "These are pretty nice, quite a step up from where Lissa lives."

"I noticed." She frowned, wondering what job Peggy Sue had gotten that allowed her to live in luxury. "Strange, since Annie claimed Peggy Sue was fired from the restaurant last week."

Max nodded but didn't respond. He went to the front door and buzzed Peggy Sue's apartment. When her voice came over the intercom, Max explained who he was. The door clicked loudly as Peggy Sue unlocked it.

Peggy Sue was waiting for them inside. She was young and scantily dressed in a miniskirt and skintight white top.

"Thanks for agreeing to meet with us," Max said, not seeming to notice the woman's attire, which belonged on a beach, not in St. Louis in November.

"No problem. Come on in. Would you like something to drink?" Peggy Sue might be a tad underdressed for November, but she was trying to be a good hostess.

"Nothing for me. We just finished eating lunch." Max took a seat on the sofa, and Tara sat beside him.

"Your message said Melissa was hurt and in the hospital ICU." Peggy Sue sat down on the chair across from them. "You think Gary put her there?"

"Yes, we do." Max's tone didn't give any room for doubt. "What can you tell me about him?"

"He seemed to have a lot of money," Peggy Sue said, reinforcing Tara's concern that money was part of the reason Melissa had gone back to him. "He was always buying Melissa gifts, jewelry, flowers, little weekend getaways."

Max's lips thinned as if he wasn't thrilled with the news. "Do you know where he worked? Or what his last name was?"

Peggy Sue lit up a cigarette and inhaled deeply. Tara swallowed her protest, since it was Peggy Sue's apartment. "No, he was pretty quiet when it came to talking about himself. I met him a couple of times, and I have to say I wasn't impressed. I mean, maybe he had some money, but with that scar of his, he wasn't very good-looking."

Max exchanged a surprised glance with her and then turned back toward Peggy Sue. "Scar? What kind of scar?"

"On his face, right here," Peggy Sue drew a scarlet-tipped nail down from the corner of the right side of her mouth down to the lower edge of her jaw. "It was deep and made him look like he was frowning."

Tara shivered a little, wondering if Gary had gotten into a fight to end up with such a disfiguring scar.

"Did he have any other distinguishing marks? Like tattoos or piercings?" Max persisted.

Peggy Sue pursed her lips thoughtfully. "I'm pretty sure he had a tattoo on his bicep, but I never saw the whole thing, so I couldn't tell you what the design was."

"Right or left arm?" Max asked.

Peggy Sue rolled her eyes. "Aren't you the picky one? How should I know? Left arm, I think. Does it matter? Isn't the scar on his face enough? There can't be that many men with a deep scar running down the side of their face."

"You've been a great help," Max said, soothing her ruffled ego. "Annie described him as having short reddish-brown hair. Is that what you remember?"

"Yes, that's right." Peggy Sue raised one eyebrow. "So, is that it? That's all you need to know? Because I have to leave soon to go to work."

"Where do you work?" Tara asked, giving in to her curiosity. "We heard you don't work at the restaurant anymore."

Peggy Sue barked out a harsh laugh. "Yeah, that's one way of putting it. The tips at that joint were peanuts compared to what I make at the strip club, so I stopped going. Too bad about Melissa being in the hospital, because I was going to put in a good word for her so she could get a job with me. I told her she didn't need Gary to buy her things, she can buy her own things once she was making more money."

Tara sucked in a harsh breath, glancing at Max, whose expression turned grim. But he didn't say anything to antagonize their hostess; he simply stood, rising to his feet. "You're right. My sister doesn't need Gary to buy her things. Thanks again for your help, Peggy Sue. We really appreciate your help with Gary."

"I feel bad about Melissa," Peggy Sue said. "Tell her to come see me when she's feeling better."

"Sure." Max smiled and held out his hand.

Peggy Sue slipped a business card into his palm as she took his hand. "Stop by later, if you have time. I'll buy you a drink."

"I don't know if I'll have time, but thanks for the offer," Max said, letting her down gently. From the mild distaste in his look, Tara didn't think he was the type who went to strip clubs.

And why that made her happy, she had no idea. He might be a nice guy, but he didn't believe in God.

They left Peggy Sue's apartment. Outside, she took a deep breath, clearing the smoke from her lungs. "She was nice in her own way," she said as they headed toward his rental car.

"At least she gave us a few more details to go by," Max agreed. "But she's crazy if she thinks I'm going to let Lissa work with her at some strip club."

While she understood his sentiments, he wasn't going to be around to control what his sister did and didn't do. "Let's not worry about that right now. Let's concentrate on finding Gary. Peggy Sue's description was helpful, but we should really try to find Melissa's cell phone, don't you think?"

"Yeah. The picture would be something to take to the cops, anyway," Max muttered, still upset by Peggy Sue's comments. "Then maybe Newton will make Lissa's case a higher priority."

"And so he should," Tara said. She wondered again about that scar. "Do you think the scar is enough to make Gary camera shy? Maybe we're wrong about him being wanted by the police."

"I don't know," Max said slowly. "Maybe. But I can't get over the idea that he's trying to lay low for some other reason than pure vanity."

She had to agree. The guy Melissa's coworkers had described didn't seem like he'd be vain about his scar. Especially not if he was throwing money around. And if he had a lot of money, why not get his scar fixed? None of this was making any sense.

Was he involved in buying or selling drugs? Was that how Melissa had met him? Even if Gary was selling drugs, that didn't exactly help as far as finding him.

When they arrived at Melissa's apartment building, Max led the way inside, using his sister's keys to unlock the front door, and then again upstairs when they reached her apartment. He had to jiggle the key a bit to get it to work, and when the door swung open, he stopped abruptly in the doorway.

Tara gasped when she saw the mess. A plant was

knocked over, the base cracked and broken, dirt spilled all over the floor. A picture of a seascape hung crookedly on the wall. A broken lamp was tipped on its side, and a rust-colored smudge on the wall next to the door looked as if it might be blood.

Melissa's blood.

She could all too easily imagine how Melissa had fought with Gary, knocking over the plant in her desperate need to get away.

A low tortured sound came from Max's throat, and Tara grabbed his arm, hoping to keep him grounded. Seeing this had to be much worse for him.

"Max, don't. We already knew Melissa was hurt here. We should have realized the place would still be a mess."

He didn't answer, didn't even glance at her. Every muscle in his body was tense as if he wanted to break away from her grasp and punch something. Or someone.

Like Gary.

"Maybe we should call the police," she said in a calm voice. "Officer Newton should see this. Maybe they can find some fingerprints here."

"He should have already seen this place, they were called to the scene when she was taken to the hospital, weren't they?" Max pointed out in a low, clipped tone.

"Yes, I guess you're right."

Finally Max's tense muscles relaxed and he took a deep breath. She was amazed at how well he'd pulled himself together. "Let's go. Watch your step," Max directed, taking her hand in his. "Try not to disturb anything."

With his help, she was able to leap over the mess in the doorway. Curiously, she glanced around. The rest of Melissa's apartment wasn't exactly neat and tidy. There were a pile of dirty dishes in the sink and an empty pizza box and beer cans strewn all over the kitchen counter. A thin layer of dust covered the surfaces.

"You take her bedroom," she suggested. "I'll take the living room and kitchen."

Max nodded. "Holler if you find her phone."

Splitting up wasn't a bad strategy, but as she poked through Melissa's things, she began to wonder if there really was a phone containing a picture of Gary. Maybe Gary had already found it and erased it? Maybe the guy really had disappeared without a trace?

The phone wasn't on any of the tables or the tiny desk littered with papers. Could the picture on the phone have been part of their fight? She sat down on the sofa, wondering if Melissa and Gary had fought after eating the pizza or if the boxes were left from days earlier.

Something small lying on the floor beside the living room table caught her eyes. She bent down and picked it up. A matchbook. The cover was embossed with the words, Under the Beam.

Melissa had mentioned Gary smoked, but she knew Melissa didn't. As she glanced around the room, there wasn't a single candle in sight.

A thrill of hope surged. This matchbook was likely left by Gary. And if so, Under the Beam might be a place where they could find him.

EIGHT

Max stared at the matchbook Tara had shown him. It was identical to the one he'd found in Lissa's purse. "Under the Beam? I've never heard of it. Have you?"

"No, I'm afraid not," she said, a frown puckered in her brow. "You don't think…" Tara's voice trailed off but, he could guess what she'd thought.

"That it's the strip club where Peggy Sue works?" he asked in a wry tone. "I don't know, maybe." He couldn't even imagine Lissa going into such a place. "Actually, to be honest, it sounds more like a pub or a restaurant than a strip club."

"Maybe the matchbook doesn't have anything to do with Gary at all," Tara murmured in a dejected tone. "I guess I was just hoping we'd find another clue since her cell phone isn't anywhere to be found."

"She had this same matchbook in her purse, so it could definitely be a clue. We have to check it out." Max didn't want to give up hope. Not yet. Even if it seemed like every time they took one step forward they slid backward for two more. "Where could her cell phone be?"

"I think Gary has it."

He had to agree. The only thing he'd found in Lissa's bedroom was the picture on her dresser. It was taken before he'd gone into the service. He and Lissa and their father were standing together, smiling brightly into the camera.

Who would have thought that merely a year later he'd be sent to Iraq and his father would die of a massive heart attack? He'd been glad to see Lissa had kept the picture, a small keepsake of happier times.

Max sank down onto the sofa next to Tara. From everything he'd heard about Lissa, she'd changed in the years he'd been gone. Or at the very least, she'd made some poor choices.

What had happened? Had being alone after their father had died been too much for her? Now more than ever he wished he could have been here for Lissa. Maybe if he had, she wouldn't be in the situation she was in.

"I think you're right," he said finally. "Gary must have taken the phone. Unless the police have it, which I think is doubtful." Newton hadn't mentioned having Lissa's phone.

"I wonder if the cell-phone picture is what started the fight?" Tara mused.

He didn't want to think about his sister being attacked by this guy. Not just once but several times. "Tara, you're Lissa's social worker, right?"

She tensed, straightening her spine. "Yes."

"Why?" He swiveled so he could look at her directly. "Why did Lissa need a social worker? Just because of the abuse?"

She bit her lip and twisted her slim, ringless fingers together. He was oddly glad she didn't still wear her dead husband's wedding ring. "I'm sorry, but I can't tell you."

His brows shot upward. "What do you mean that you can't tell me?"

"Max." She lifted a pleading gaze to his. "Please don't ask me. I'm bound by the federal privacy laws to keep all personal client information confidential, so I can't tell you."

He clenched his fingers, taking a deep breath to remain calm. So what if Tara was bound by the government's privacy laws? This was his sister's life they were fighting for. He couldn't believe she'd let him run into one dead end after another, when she might know something that could help them.

He glanced over at her, only slightly mollified when he saw the troubled anxiety in her eyes. She was clearly torn between duty to her job and wanting to help him.

"Tara, I need you to tell me if there is any information that you have about Lissa that will help me find Gary."

Her torturous expression made him feel guilty. "I don't think so."

"That's not good enough," he snapped, losing his temper. "I need to know for certain that you're not jeopardizing my investigation."

"Your investigation? I thought this was a police matter." Tara rose to her feet and took several steps, putting distance between them.

Did she expect him to lash out physically like Gary did? The thought deflated his anger like a popped balloon.

"I can't tell you any details about your sister's case—end of discussion. Are you ready to go? Or do you want to look around the apartment some more?"

He dropped his head into his hands and took several deep breaths. "I'm sorry," he muttered, feeling like a lowlife for even giving the impression he was anything like Gary. "I didn't mean to scare you."

"Scare me?" she echoed in a confused tone. "What are you talking about? Max?" She waited for him to look at her. "Did you really think I was afraid of you just because you were upset with me?"

"I don't know," he admitted. "I shouldn't have lost my temper like that."

"We're both under a fair amount of stress right now. I think you're entitled to get upset on occasion."

Tara was really something. Not only wasn't she angry with him but she let him off the hook much quicker than he deserved. He glanced down at the matchbook. Under the Beam. He needed her cell phone, with a number or a picture of Gary. Something solid he could take to Newton to jump-start the investigation, not a matchbook that could mean nothing.

"Let's go," he said, standing and heading toward the door. "We can use the computer at the hotel to do a search on this place."

"Max." Tara stayed where she was, between the sofa and the desk. He glanced over his shoulder at her. Her gaze was pleading. "You need to understand that if it comes down to a matter of life or death I will tell you what I know."

He stared at her for a long moment, before giving a brief nod. "I'll hold you to that promise."

Tara was exhausted. The short catnap she'd taken in the car earlier hadn't been enough. She hadn't gone so long without sleep since Ted's illness.

Remembering how she'd woken up to find Max's face hovering over her made her cheeks flush. Had he watched her sleep for long? How embarrassing.

Max's phone rang again, and she wondered who the caller was this time. She was surprised when he handed the phone to her. "It's for you."

"For me?" She lifted the cell phone to her ear. "Hello?"

"Ms. Carmichael? Detective Graham here. We have Tyrone Adams in custody. Will you come down to the station for a few minutes?"

"I think I can. Just a minute." She put her hand over the speaker and turned to Max. "They have Tyrone in custody and want me to come down to the station."

Max didn't hesitate. "Tell him we'll be there in ten minutes."

She repeated what Max had said, before closing the phone and handing it back to him. "I wonder why they want me to come down to the station."

Max shrugged and slid the cell phone back into his pocket. "I don't know. Maybe they need you to validate pieces of his story. He is your client, after all."

Maybe, although she hadn't seen Tyrone since he'd failed his random drug test. He'd wanted her to lie for him. Of course she'd refused. "Sometimes I wonder if I really do any of my clients any good," she murmured.

Max shot her a surprised glance. "What makes you say that?"

Wallowing in self-pity wasn't like her, so she tried to snap out of it. Melissa's and Tyrone's failures weren't her fault. "Never mind. Just a moment of weakness."

The downtown police station wasn't far. She walked in, feeling a bit apprehensive. Detective Graham came to meet her and then escorted her over to a one-way mirror overlooking one of the interrogation rooms. Inside, Tyrone Adams sat slouched in his chair, flanked by officers Anderson and Schimberg.

"He doesn't have a solid alibi for Friday night during the time frame between when your dog was drugged and the bomb was placed in your house," Detective Graham explained. "Claimed he was with a bunch of his loser friends, but I'm sure they'd lie to cover for him. He can't give me the name of any reliable adult who be able to verify they saw him that night."

Her stomach churned as she watched the police officers continue to question Tyrone. Suddenly he got angry and sat up straight, saying something defiant to the officers. Now that she was looking at him sitting in the chair, she realized he was much shorter than she'd realized. "I don't think that's him," she said, casting a concerned glance at Max. "He's too short to be the guy we saw behind the wheel of the brown car."

Max nodded slowly. "You're right. He is definitely much shorter than the guy we saw in the car." He turned toward Detective Graham. "Did you find Steve Jasper yet?"

"No, we're working on that now. It's only been what, a couple hours since you faxed the list over to us? Our attention up until today has been focused on this one here." He indicated Tyrone Adams with the jerk of his thumb. "You're sure he's not the one who's been following you?"

"I'm sorry," Tara said lifting her shoulders helplessly. "But I really don't think so."

"All right," Detective Graham said with a heavy sigh. "I was going to ask how well you knew his loser friends, since he gave me a list, but I guess it doesn't matter now. We'll have to let him go and work on finding this guy, Jasper, instead."

"I wish I could do more to help," Tara murmured.

"You're doing fine," Max surprised her by saying, flashing a gentle smile. "Once they pick up Jasper, this will likely be over. I have a strong hunch he's your guy."

He could be right. She turned to the detective. "Is there a way to find out if my checking account has been tampered with?"

"Your checking account?" Max echoed incredulously. "What do you mean?"

"Remember when I went to the hospital ATM?" she asked. "Well, there wasn't any money in my checking account. And I know there wasn't a lot to start, but I'm sure there was at least five hundred sixty dollars. I couldn't even take out twenty—the message kept reading Insufficient Funds."

"We can look into it," Detective Graham said, scratching his jaw with a frown. "Are you saying your stalker accessed your bank account?"

"I don't know. I guess it's not too likely. Maybe it is some sort of bank error."

"The guy was in her house," Max pointed out. "It's not that much of a stretch to think he'd copied down her bank-account information and figured out a way to hack into it."

"A hacker?" Detective Graham raised a brow. "Not exactly the profile of your average stalker."

"Yeah, well, I don't think your average stalker blows up their victim's house, either," Max said dryly. "This guy isn't just obsessed. He wants to hurt her. He's looking for some sort of revenge."

"All right, tell me about this Steve Jasper," Detective Graham said, turning toward Tara. "Why do you suddenly think he's the guy who's been stalking you?"

"I met him a few years ago. He had a ten-year-old daughter, Stacey, who was reported by the school as having suspicious bruises," Tara said, repeating the story for the detective. "I was the social worker assigned to Stacey's case, so I went to their house for a home visit. Just watching Stacey interact with her father made me suspicious. She watched him warily, as if expecting him to lash out at any moment. She jumped like he'd shocked her, nearly tripping over her feet in her anxiety to do what he'd asked."

"You think Jasper was beating his daughter?" Detective Graham asked, cutting to the heart of the matter.

"Yes." Even now, two years later, there was no doubt in her mind about that. "I went back for a second follow-up visit, unannounced as we're instructed to do, and I could hear him screaming at her before I even got up to the door. She was crying when I arrived, and her cheek was bright red as if he'd slapped her. I took Stacey away right then and there. A couple days later, I had to appear in court to testify as to why we'd removed the girl from his custody."

"Tell him the rest," Max urged when she stopped.

She took a deep breath. "Mr. Jasper lost his temper in the courtroom after I gave my testimony. I don't know if he was drinking or on drugs, but he screamed at me, like he'd screamed at his daughter the day I showed up at their house. He threatened to kill me. The police arrested him at the time, but I thought it might be possible he's out on parole by now."

"Hmm. That would explain why he waited so long to go after you," Detective Graham grudgingly admitted. "You're right. Jasper is a strong possibility. We'll get working on finding this guy right away. Should be easy enough to make sure he's not still doing jail time."

"Thanks," she said, relieved to have everything out in the open. "I appreciate your help. And I'm sorry about Tyrone. At the time I really thought he might be a suspect."

"Don't worry about it." Detective Graham waved a hand. "The important thing here is that we find this guy before he lashes out at anyone else."

"I agree, but Tara's safety is the primary concern," Max added. "So far, we don't know that he's taken his anger out on anyone else."

Detective Graham's eyes narrowed, as if he didn't appreciate Max telling him how to do his job. "But now that you're doing such a good job of hiding Ms. Carmichael, he's bound to be frustrated and angry. There's no doubt in my mind that he's a threat to the public, as well. We'll get him," he added, turning toward Tara. "We'll be in touch."

"Okay." Tara tried to smile. She caught one last look at Tyrone, who was sitting with his head buried in his hands. The poor kid must have been shaken by being picked up by the police and brought down here. The social-worker part of her wanted to talk to Tyrone, to see how he was doing, but this was hardly the time or the place.

Max was quiet as they made their way back to the car. Darkness had fallen, the days much shorter now with winter approaching. She glanced at Max's strong profile, wondering what he was thinking. He seemed so certain Steve Jasper was guilty, but she'd already been wrong about Tyrone. What if she was wrong about Steve, too? She didn't like the idea she was adding to their problems by claiming they might be her stalker.

The wind picked up, sending a sharp cold breeze over her. She shivered, ducking into the warmth of Max's rental car.

"Why didn't you tell me?" hc asked as he pulled away from the curb, merging into traffic.

"Tell you what? About my checking account?"

"Yeah." Max's expression was impossible to read in the dark. "You told me the machine was broken."

"I know. I'm sorry. I honestly thought the machine was broken at first, or that I was losing my mind, forgetting how much money I had in my account. But as the day went on, I kept thinking about it, mentally retracing the various things I bought, and soon realized the discrepancy might not be just my imagination."

"And you didn't think it was important enough to mention?" he asked, skeptically.

"I was going to tell you at lunch, but we were interrupted by Annie," she said a little defensively. "At that moment, finding Gary was more important than my problems."

Max was silent for a moment. "Nothing is more important than your safety, Tara," he said in a serious tone. "Nothing. Please remember that the next time it seems like I'm not listening to you."

A warm flush crept into her cheeks at his caring attitude. This was obviously his way of declaring a truce after their earlier argument. She shouldn't read too much into his sincere tone. This was just his way of being nice.

She'd truly felt horrible that she'd been unable to

give Max the information he'd so desperately wanted about Melissa. But then again, he wouldn't be at all happy to know the full extent of trouble his sister had gotten into. In some respects, working as a waitress in a strip club was nothing compared to drug abuse.

She'd tried to get Melissa back on track. And she had quit drugs but then had gotten tangled up with Gary.

"Are we heading back to the hotel?" she asked, changing the subject. "We still need to research Under the Beam. I was thinking we could just look it up in the phone book. Not every place has a Web site, but they should all be listed in the phone directory."

"True," he agreed slowly. "I guess I will head back. Do you mind eating dinner at the hotel?"

"Of course I don't mind. Whatever is easier for you is fine with me." She hesitated, and then added, "I want you to know, Max, that once this is all over I will pay you back for everything you've done for me. I'm really not trying to take advantage of your kindness."

"Tara, have I given you the impression that I need payment?" Max asked with a hint of exasperation. "Because that's not true at all. In fact, in some ways I'm taking advantage of you. Going through this alone would be much worse. I'm glad you're here with me. I'm not helping you out because I expect something in return. Knowing you were here for my sister while I was gone is enough for me."

"All right, I won't mention it again." She dropped the issue for now, even though she could have pointed out that working with his sister was part of her job.

Once they found Gary, and Max headed back to Iraq, she vowed to do a better job with Melissa. This time, she wouldn't just treat Max's sister like a client. She'd reach out as a friend.

"Let's eat first," Max suggested. "Then research the matchbook."

She didn't protest when he led the way into the tiny dining room. The fare was simple, but she didn't mind. She'd never acquired a taste for fancy food anyway.

They gave their order to the waitress. Distracted, Max stared off into the distance, as if he'd forgotten she was there. Something was bothering him.

"What is it?" she asked, a little disconcerted that she was so in tune to his emotions after only knowing him for twenty-four hours.

"Peggy Sue's description of Gary has been bugging me," he admitted. "The scar and the tattoo. Reminds me of a guy I knew a few years ago in Iraq who got a similar scar on his face during a tussle with an Iraqi hostile."

"Really?" She leaned forward. "Do you think it's the same man?"

Max frowned and shook his head. "I can't see how it could be the same guy. Shortly after I was promoted to lieutenant, I found him taking his bitter anger out on our Iraqi prisoners so I had him arrested." His expression turned grim. "Last I knew Billy was serving time in Leavenworth for his crimes."

NINE

Max hadn't thought about Billy in a long time. The soldier had given the U.S. a bad name in Baghdad, during a time they very much needed the cooperation of the local citizens.

Billy had blamed all Iraqis for his disfiguring scar. He'd taken too much pleasure in strong-arming the prisoners. And he'd blamed Max for turning him in.

"So his name is Billy, not Gary," Tara said with a sigh.

Not exactly. He rubbed his jaw. "Actually, his name was Garth Williams, but he preferred to be called Billy. Rumor had it that Billy's mother divorced his father, leaving Billy with his dad while she went on to pursue a country-music career. Which might explain some of the animosity toward his given name."

"Garth? Gary? They really could be the same guy," Tara said eagerly. "If he's not still in Leavenworth."

"I'll make a few phone calls to make sure," Max agreed slowly. "Although I can't believe he would have gotten out this soon."

"And it would be quite a coincidence that he ended up here in St. Louis, dating your sister," Tara mused.

Max scowled. He didn't believe in coincidences—especially not this one. Had Billy come here on purpose? He'd know Max was still in the military, though, wouldn't he? So what was the reason Billy had come here?

He pulled out his cell phone to see if he could reach his commanding officer, but it rang before he could punch in the number. Surprised, he answered, "Hello?"

"Lieutenant Forrester? This is Dr. Kappel from St. Louis General Hospital. I'm afraid your sister has taken a turn for the worse. Are you somewhere nearby? I'd like you to come in as soon as possible. I need your consent to take her for emergency surgery."

"I'm across the street. I'll be right there," Max said quickly, pushing away from the table so fast he knocked his chair over.

"What's wrong?" Tara asked, jumping to her feet taking the time to pick up his chair.

He threw down enough money to cover the tab and grabbed Tara's hand. "We have to go. Lissa has taken a turn for the worse. They want my permission to take her for emergency surgery."

"Lieutenant Forrester?" Dr. Kappel glanced over at them when they walked in.

"Yes." Max looked up at the monitor over Lissa's bed, but he couldn't really make sense of the numbers. He returned the doctor's handshake. "Tell me what's going on with Lissa."

Dr. Kappel glanced at Tara. "Is it okay for me to go into detail in front of your companion?"

"Yes." Max's impatience got the best of him. "You think Lissa needs surgery?"

"We've been monitoring your sister's intracranial pressure, and it's been going up all afternoon. Now it's at a dangerously high level. I'd like to take her to surgery in order to remove the blood clot that's formed in her brain to see if that helps relieve the pressure."

"But isn't there a chance the surgery alone could cause her brain to swell, too?" Tara asked.

Max glanced at her gratefully. His medical knowledge was very limited.

"There is a risk, yes," Dr. Kappel admitted. "But quite honestly, the risk of not doing anything is higher than if we operate. Her intracranial pressure is already dangerously high. If we don't do anything, there's a very good chance all the blood supply will be cut off from her brain and she'll die."

Lissa couldn't die. She was too young. How could this have happened? Remembering the violent scene inside her apartment made a red haze of fury cloud his vision.

If Billy had done this to Lissa, he wouldn't rest until he'd hunted the man down with or without the help of the authorities.

"The decision is yours, Lieutenant Forrester," Dr. Kappel reminded him.

"Take her to surgery," Max said in a voice hoarse with emotion.

His words spurred the health care team into immediate action. The surgeon made him sign the consent form while the nurses quickly disconnected Lissa from the monitors. In less than five minutes, they were ready to go.

Max barely had time to bend over and press a kiss against Lissa's forehead before they whisked her away. He stared blindly after them, and then the pressure became too much. He needed to be alone. He spun on his heel and stalked away.

The hospital corridors were relatively empty this late at night. Without realizing it, he found himself heading down to the hospital chapel, located not far from the first-floor lobby.

He wasn't sure why he'd come. He didn't know what to say or if any prayer he might offer would even be heard.

God had turned his back on his soldiers. On Keith. Good men who'd lost their lives in battle. Why hadn't their prayers been heard? Why would God listen to him now?

There was no answer. Silence filled the chapel.

A muffled sound caught his attention. He turned to glance behind him, not surprised to see Tara hovering in the doorway, her expression full of hope.

"I haven't been to church in over four years," he said in a low voice. Better for Tara to understand that his being here wasn't a major revelation or anything.

"Understandable since you've been in Iraq for a majority of the time," she said, coming over to sit beside him.

"No, it's more than that. It's been difficult to believe. To have faith. My best friend, Keith, died in my arms despite my prayers..." His voice trailed off. He could still see Keith's pain-ravaged face, his buddy's concern over leaving his wife and son when he knew he wasn't going to make it.

"I felt the same way after Ted died," she admitted softly. "He was so young, and we'd only been married a couple months when he was diagnosed with pancreatic cancer. At the time, I just couldn't understand why God was taking him away from me."

He couldn't imagine how difficult that must have been for her. "Yet you still believe," he said, making it a statement, not a question.

Her smile was lopsided. "Yes. I do. I won't lie to you, Max. There are times I still struggle with losing Ted, but deep down I know God has a reason for taking my husband. I might not understand the reason, but that doesn't negate the fact that it exists."

"How can you be so sure?" Max asked, unable to mask his lingering despair. "It doesn't seem fair for good people like Keith, or my sister or your husband to suffer, while others don't."

She leaned forward and took his hand in hers, as if willing him to believe like she did. "I believe Ted is in a much better place, Max. And so is Keith. Don't you remember what the Bible says? 'I say to you, he who hears My Word and believes in Him who sent Me has everlasting life, and shall not come into judgment, but has passed from death into life.'"

Everlasting life. The words were familiar from church services he'd attended long ago. "I used to believe in heaven," he said. "But it's hard when you look into the face of death over and over again. I just can't help feeling angry at God, rather than looking to Him for support."

"It's never too late, Max," she said, her tone earnest. "God is always there for you. All you have to do is open your heart and your mind. Listen and pray."

He couldn't help responding to her. "You make it sound so easy."

"Because it is." She tilted her head toward him. "You don't have to carry your burdens all alone, Max."

Maybe she was right. Maybe it was time to stop blaming God and look to Him for strength, instead. That's what Tara had obviously done. To have buried a husband so young, she must have gotten her strength and courage from somewhere. Why not from God?

God might not answer his prayer, but it wouldn't be for his lack of trying. Closing his eyes, Max reached out with his heart and his mind.

"Please, God, take care of Lissa. Help heal her injuries and give her a second chance to do better. Thank You. Amen."

"Amen," Tara echoed, and to his embarrassment, he'd realized he'd spoken the prayer out loud.

Tara smiled at him, her gaze so full of hope and admiration that he couldn't find any room for regrets. Instead, he basked in her glowing attention, realizing in that moment that what he felt for Tara was much different than what he'd felt for Clare.

He shied away from the notion. He was physically tired and emotionally drained. Maybe he shared a special bond with Tara, but that was only because they'd spent the better part of the day together, partners in their search for Gary.

"Maybe you should head back to the hotel," he said, giving her the opportunity to leave, since her face was deeply lined with exhaustion. "It's late, but I'm going to stick around for a while yet, until Lissa comes out of surgery."

"Then I'm staying here with you," Tara said firmly, covering a yawn. "Let's just call up to the ICU to let them know where we are."

"Good idea." He didn't deserve Tara's friendship. But he wasn't strong enough to send her away, either. "Okay. We'll wait together."

She made the phone call and then came back to sit beside him. She took his hand in hers, clasping it tightly, and rested her head against his shoulder, as if content to stay there with him forever.

Suddenly, being in the hospital chapel didn't seem so bad.

It was close to midnight before they heard news about Melissa. Tara had fallen asleep leaning against Max, but he gently shook her awake when Dr. Kappel came looking for them.

Groggy, she rubbed the gritty sleep from her eyes. The neurosurgeon looked exhausted but satisfied. "Melissa came through the surgery just fine, and so far her intracranial pressure numbers have dropped considerably. It's too early to say for sure, but at this point, we're hopeful the surgery has been a success."

"Thank You, Lord," she whispered. Glancing up at Max, she could see the relief in his eyes, as well.

"Yes," he murmured, as if agreeing with her prayer of thanks. He reached a hand out to the surgeon. "Thanks, Dr. Kappel."

"You're welcome." He gestured to the doorway. "You can go up to see your sister if you like. The nurses are just getting her settled."

Max hesitated glancing down at her. "Let's go see Lissa, just for a few minutes."

"All right." He swept one last glance around the chapel before heading for the door.

They didn't speak on the way up to see Melissa. There really wasn't any need for words. It was strange how peaceful she felt being with Max. And she was thrilled to know Max hadn't completely turned his back on God.

This was her mission, she knew it deep in her heart. God wanted her to lead Max back into the church. A mission she gladly accepted.

When they reached Melissa's room, Max frowned. "She doesn't look any better," he said.

"I know. But look at her heart monitor." Tara indicated the numbers running down the right side of the monitor. She'd spent some time in the hospital, enough to learn just a few of the basics. "See the number fourteen here?" She pointed to the bottom number.

"Before surgery it was reading close to thirty. Now it's less than half that high. She is better, even though you can't see any physical changes."

"I guess you're right," Max said with a weary sigh. "I can't expect miracles overnight, I guess."

"No. You just need to have faith." She didn't want to preach anymore at him tonight. He'd already come a long way.

"Just give me a minute, and then we'll go back to the hotel," he said, stepping closer to his sister's bedside.

She stepped back toward the door. "Take all the time you need," she assured him.

It was too late to do any searching for Under the Beam. Max walked her to her hotel-room door. He pinned her with an intense look. For a moment she wondered if he might kiss her, but he didn't make a move. "Good night, Tara."

"Good night, Max." Swallowing a tiny spurt of disappointment, she opened the door and sent him one last smile before closing it behind her.

After getting ready to go to sleep, she climbed into bed and prepared to pray. "Dear Lord, thank You for showing me the way to help Max believe. Thanks also for keeping Melissa safe in Your care. Amen."

Now that she knew Max was at the core of her mission, she didn't mind when his face lingered in her head as she drifted off to sleep.

Her lack of sleep the night before must have caught up with her, because she overslept. When Max tapped at their connecting door, she blinked, realizing the time was already close to nine-thirty in the morning.

She scrambled out of bed, yelping when she stubbed her toe on the desk in her rush to get ready. It was Sunday, and she wanted to go to church. Since she wasn't familiar with the area, she'd thought it would be nice to attend the eleven o'clock service in the hospital chapel.

"I just woke up," she called through the door. "I need to take a shower. I'll call you when I'm finished."

"Okay," Max replied. "I'll be here when you're ready."

He sounded like he was in good spirits. Had he called the hospital already? Maybe Melissa was doing better this morning. She was feeling pretty cheerful herself. Today was the day Beau would be released from the veterinary hospital. She was so glad he was doing all right. She needed to talk to Max about whether or not the hotel would allow pets; if not, she could always take him to Mrs. Henderson's house, although she'd rather keep Beau with her.

She and Beau had been through a lot together. Especially after Ted died.

She finished her shower in record time. She quickly blow-dried her hair and then spent a few extra minutes to weave the strands of it into a neat and tidy French braid.

When she was finished, she picked up her purse and her key. "Max?" she called through the connecting door. "I'm ready. Meet me in the hallway, all right?"

"Sure thing."

She hoped none of the other hotel patrons could hear their conversation through the connecting door. Max met her in the hallway, and they walked down to the lobby together.

"Do you think we should ask the manager if they allow pets?" she asked in a whisper.

"We can ask," Max agreed. "But don't get your hopes up. Don't worry. If they won't allow pets, we'll look for another place to stay."

How sweet. But she was also a little worried about being gone all day, the way they were yesterday, and leaving her dog alone. "That's all right. I think I can get Mrs. Henderson to watch him."

"We'll talk it over at breakfast," Max said. "I called the hospital first thing this morning, and apparently Lissa is doing pretty well. Her intracranial pressure numbers stayed down all night."

"Oh, Max, that's wonderful news." Between Melissa and Beau, this day couldn't get much better. She smiled at him. "I think maybe our prayers have been answered."

Max didn't tense up or look away. This time, he looked straight into her eyes and smiled back at her. "You could be right."

"I hope you don't mind if we go to the eleven-o'clock service in the chapel," she added. "I thought staying there would be more convenient, since we'll be at the hospital anyway."

After a slight hesitation, he nodded. "Sure. If that's what you want."

She didn't let his lack of enthusiasm bother her. She

was so happy she wanted to skip all the way to the hospital. But she kept her emotions in check. After all, they still had a lot of work to do in order to find Gary.

"Have you gotten in touch with your commanding officer yet?" she asked, as they waited for the elevator. "To see if Garth Williams is still in Leavenworth?"

"Not yet, although I left him a message early this morning," Max informed her. "I sure hope he calls me back soon."

"He will," she said confidently. "I have a good feeling that we're on the right track."

"Oh you do, huh?" Max said with a teasing smile. "Obviously, getting a night of decent sleep seems to have done wonders for you."

She wanted to tell him that her cheerful mood had more to do with him agreeing to attend church with her, but they'd already arrived at Melissa's room.

There was a new nurse at Melissa's bedside, who introduced herself as Emma. She told them Melissa was doing well, her intracranial pressures were staying well below twenty, which is what they wanted to hear.

"How long before you ease up on the medication?" Max asked.

"Generally, we wait a few days, just to make sure she's past the peak of her brain swelling. If she's doing this well by Tuesday, I'm sure the doctor will start weaning her medications."

Max spent a few minutes by his sister's bedside. When it was time for the church service, he went with her, like he promised.

The service was shorter than a normal church service, but just being in the calm atmosphere of the chapel helped fill her with God's peace. And she was happy that Max stood solemnly beside her the whole time even if he didn't voice any prayers.

When the service was over, they walked back across the street to the hotel to pick up Max's rental car.

"How about we stop for a meal first?" Max asked. "All we had were a few muffins from the hotel, and it's almost lunchtime."

"Couldn't we pick up something after we pick up Beau?" she asked plaintively. "I miss him."

"All right," he agreed with a resigned sigh. "After we pick up Beau."

She couldn't wait to see her dog. The ride to the veterinary hospital didn't take too long. It wasn't that far from her house, and when she went inside, the kind vet welcomed her.

Since she didn't have any cash, she put the vet's bill on her credit card, breathing a sigh of relief when that wasn't rejected. She must not have reached her limit yet.

"Beau!" Her little dog barked excitedly when he saw her, and she gave him a big hug, laughing as he licked her face. "Thanks again," she said to the vet.

"You're welcome. He might be a little sluggish yet, but I'm sure he'll be back to his normal playful self soon."

Beau didn't move as fast as he normally did. Of course, he had to stop and sniff at Max's shoes first, wagging his tail in welcome.

Beau trotted by her side all the way out the door. And then something must have set him off, because suddenly he barked ferociously, leaping forward and straining at the end of the leash, knocking her off balance to the point she almost tripped and fell.

"Beau! What's wrong with you?" she asked with exasperation, bending over to get a better grip on the dog. So much for being sluggish.

"Get down!" Max roared, tackling her with a low hit, sending them both crashing to the ground with enough force to knock the breath from her body.

TEN

Someone was shooting at Tara!

Heart lodged in his throat, Max struggled to remain calm. This wasn't a flashback. This was real.

"Max? What's going on?" Tara asked in a muffled voice. "Get off me."

"Stay down." Using his cell phone he dialed 911. "Gunshots fired at the corner of Pine and Reese outside the emergency veterinary hospital."

"Is anyone hurt?" the dispatcher asked.

"Not yet. But hurry."

Beau was growling, but thankfully Tara had maintained a tight hold on his leash. They needed to move. Even down on the ground like this, they were too exposed.

"Max." Tara squirmed beneath him. "I can't breathe."

"Sorry." He levered upright but kept his head down. He lifted Tara off the ground and half dragged her around the corner of the building, Beau trailing on his leash behind them. He plastered her against the wall, staying in front of her, hiding her slender frame behind his larger one.

He wasn't leaving her unprotected for anything.

"Did you say shots fired?" Tara asked in a trembling voice, pulling Beau so he was close to their feet. "I thought that noise was a car backfiring."

"Beau saved your life, barking like that. The shot missed by scant inches when you ducked, although there's a nice round bullet hole in the brick building," he said. "I'm betting from an AK-47 rifle."

"A rifle?" her voice rose to a squeak. A shiver rippled over her skin. He longed to reassure her, but he couldn't.

They weren't out of danger yet.

Max tensed, scanning the area, wishing he had a weapon. The shot had come from across the street, but the shooter could right now be making his way around the building to take another shot at them. Any minute, he expected a bullet to slam into him.

He strained to listen, trying to hear the man's movements, but the area around the veterinary hospital was eerily silent.

"What's taking the police so long to respond?" Tara whispered.

Finally the wail of police sirens filled the air. He didn't let down his guard, though, until the area was blocked off by two police cars and an ambulance.

"Are you both all right?" the first cop on the scene asked.

"I think so." Max turned to look down at Tara. Her

wide, frightened eyes and pale, pinched skin only fueled his anger.

That had been too close.

"Are you sure you heard a shot?" a second officer asked.

Wordlessly, he brushed past the police to round the corner of the building, finding the spot where Tara had been standing. He slid his hand over the smooth surface of the brick until he found the gouge.

"Here's where the slug is imbedded," he informed the cops.

They couldn't deny the evidence. One cop went to work with a knife to dig out the bullet, and the other took him aside to ask a barrage of questions. He was separated from Tara, no doubt to see if their stories matched.

When he was finished, the cop walked over to Tara, to take her statement. Moments later, more cops showed up, fanning out to investigate the area.

Feeling helpless, he made a few phone calls while he waited to hear what they uncovered.

"Did you find anything?" the first officer asked.

"Nope. There's a spot across the street beneath a big oak tree where the leaves look to be matted down. The shooter might have stood there," the second officer answered.

Max glanced over to the spot he'd indicated, judging the distance to be possible. Realizing how close the guy had been made the hair on the back of his neck stand up.

"Canvass the area. Someone must have saw or heard something." The cop turned to Max. "Why is someone shooting at you?"

"Actually I'm pretty sure he was shooting at me," Tara said softly, stepping forward and hanging on to Beau's leash with a deathlike grip. Surprisingly the dog wasn't barking at the police, not the way he'd gone crazy when they'd walked out of the building.

Max filled them in on the details of Tara's stalker, suggesting they get in touch with Detective Graham as soon as possible.

"Can't you two stay out of trouble for one day?" Graham asked a short while later when he arrived at the crime scene. Max figured he was a little cranky at having been called into work on a Sunday.

"Oh sure. We planned this just to ruin your day," Max said dryly. "After all, we just love getting shot at."

Graham ignored his sarcasm and scanned the area. "Why here? And why is he suddenly using a gun?"

Good questions. Max had wondered the same thing himself. He shook his head. "I don't know. It's bothering me that he only took one shot, even though he had time to take another. We were exposed for a good thirty seconds."

"Detective Graham is right. Why here? How could he have known Beau was here?" Tara asked.

"Maybe he followed us that first night," Max mused. "Or he simply watched us drive away with Beau, figuring we'd go to the closest vet." The thought that Tara's stalker was watching them that

closely made his gut churn. He'd nearly failed to protect Tara.

Graham scrubbed his jaw, his expression perplexed.
"He escalated from slashing tires to planting a bomb,
and now he's taking potshots from a distance? I don't
get it. This guy's actions aren't making a whole lot of
sense."

No, they weren't. And Max didn't like it—not one
bit. "I need to get Tara someplace safe," he said finally.
"Is there anything else you need from us?"

"No, we'll take it from here," Graham assured him.
"But you need to know that we haven't found Steve
Jasper yet. Tara was right. He'd done jail time and was
released on parole just four weeks ago. He's supposed
to meet with his parole officer on Monday morning.
We're planning to be there to greet him."

"Good." Monday wasn't soon enough, but at least
the cops had a plan. With any luck, Jasper would be in
police custody soon.

He'd been bold to risk shooting at them now. Did he
know the police were looking for him? Was this his last
chance to exact his revenge on Tara?

Max ushered Tara and Beau to his rental car. "What
do you want to do about Beau? I checked with the hotel
while you were giving your statement to the police and
they won't allow pets."

"I think we'd better take him to Mrs. Henderson's
house," Tara murmured. "Although I'm afraid my
stalker will know to look for him there."

"He shot at you, Tara, not your dog. Poisoning Beau

was just a means to an end, because he wanted to get inside your house to plant the bomb. I don't think Beau is the one in danger here."

"I suppose you're right." Her expression didn't look convincing.

"I can look for a pet-friendly hotel," Max offered, even though he really wanted to get in touch with his commanding officer. And search for a place called Under the Beam.

Gary's trail was already growing cold.

"No, Mrs. Henderson's is fine."

After dropping off the dog and watching Tara's tearful goodbye, Max headed for the hotel. No matter what Tara said, she was clearly shaken by what had happened.

She deserved a little peace and quiet.

As he drove, he glanced at her. She seemed lost in her thoughts, barely noticing where he was taking her. When they reached the hotel, he walked with her up to their rooms.

"Get some rest," he advised, pausing outside her door. "I need to make a few phone calls, since I haven't heard back from my commanding officer, yet. I promise I won't leave without letting you know."

Tara looked in his eyes. "I'm scared," she admitted.

"Please don't be afraid." Max gently smoothed her hair away from her cheek. She looked so shattered that he wanted nothing more than to put her at ease. "You're safe here with me."

He wanted very badly to kiss her. To take her into

his arms and protect her forever. The knowledge shook him to the core.

Even after what happened with Clare, he'd gone ahead and made the same mistake again.

He was falling in love with Tara.

Tara stared deep into Max's eyes, longing for something she couldn't name. Hastily, she stepped away from him, breaking the tension shimmering between them. She needed to pull herself together.

God was watching over her. She had no reason to be afraid.

"I think I will rest for a while," she said, taking her plastic room key from her purse. "I'll talk to you later."

Max gazed at her with an inscrutable expression clouding his eyes. She summoned a small smile and let herself into her hotel room.

Tossing her key and purse on the bed, she took a deep, cleansing breath. She'd been so happy earlier that morning, after attending the chapel service with Max. And picking up Beau, seeing her puppy alive and well had lifted her spirits immensely.

But those moments Max knocked her to the ground replayed over and over in her head. Listening to his terse voice telling her to stay down. She couldn't fail to notice how he'd stayed protectively in front of her, until the police arrived.

There was no doubt in her mind he would have given up his life to protect her. The humbling thought weakened her knees.

She was beginning to care for him too much. He was her mission, nothing more. A friend helping another in need.

He'd be back in Iraq soon enough, anyway.

Yet the longing in her heart wouldn't be ignored. Her emotions were in complete turmoil. She wasn't sure what to do. Having a little distance from Max should have helped put everything in perspective, but she could hear him moving about the room next door.

She longed to go to him—to stay in the safe haven of his arms.

Knowing such thoughts betrayed her love for Ted, she closed her eyes and tried to rest. But ended up praying instead.

"Thank you for keeping us safe. I've accepted Max as my mission, Lord, but please help me stay true to Ted. I promised to love him forever." There was a tiny catch in her voice as her eyes filled with tears. "Don't let me forget Ted."

She must have fallen asleep after all, because the next time she opened her eyes, the room was dim. The sun sat low on the horizon.

Walking over to the connecting door, she pressed her ear to the smooth surface. She couldn't hear anything. Had Max left? No, he'd promised not to leave without telling her.

She sensed Max was a man of his word.

Tentatively, she knocked. "Max? Are you in there?"

There was a scraping noise and then Max's reassuring voice. "I'm here. How are you feeling?"

"Hungry," she said, rubbing her stomach. They hadn't eaten all day.

"Meet me in the hall," Max said. "We'll eat, and I'll update you on what I discovered."

She took the time to quickly rebraid her hair and then met him in the hallway. His gaze swept over her. "Are you really doing all right?"

"I'm fine." She didn't want to rehash her troubled thoughts. "Tell me what you found."

Max placed a hand in the small of her back as they walked down to the lobby. She was hyperaware of his warm fingers through her sweater and the heady scent of his aftershave.

"I finally got a hold of my commanding officer. He confirmed that Billy, Garth Williams, did get out of prison early. Apparently he negotiated a shorter sentence in return for providing evidence against another soldier—someone they'd suspected in another crime."

She sucked in a quick breath at the news. "So Gary could be Garth Williams."

"As much as I hate to admit it, yes." Down in the lobby, Max hesitated. "Would you mind if we went to the hospital cafeteria instead? I haven't seen Lissa since this morning."

Because of her. She suppressed a wave of guilt. She hadn't asked for the stalker to shoot at her. "Of course not."

Soon they were seated in the noisy and surprisingly crowded cafeteria.

"I also found Under the Beam," Max said. She had

to lean forward in order to hear him. "It's a tavern, located in East St. Louis."

East St. Louis was the shady side of town.

"I think you should take this information to the police," Tara said. "I mean, really, they should be the ones looking for Gary, not you."

Max stared at her for a moment, clearly not thrilled with the idea. "I'm not sure I should tell them about Garth Williams," he argued. "We don't have solid proof he's Gary."

"What are the odds that two men have the same, disfiguring scar running down from the corner of their mouth?" she asked in exasperation. "Tell them. At least then they'll have something to go on."

"You're right," Max muttered, lifting a hand in surrender. "Okay, I'll tell them."

Satisfied with his concession, she relaxed back against the chair, gazing around the cafeteria. There were a group of nurses she recognized as working in the ICU. She hoped Melissa was continuing to improve since her surgery.

She was about to ask Max if he'd talked to the nurses when a flash of blue caught her eye. Glancing over toward the side of the cafeteria closest to the door, she saw a man dressed in a navy blue jacket and a blue baseball cap on his head. His face was shadowed, but he seemed to be looking directly at her.

Her stalker? Here?

"Max, look. See the guy in the blue baseball cap? That's him!"

The guy must have sensed they saw him, because he abruptly stood and headed for the doorway.

"Let's go," Max jumped to his feet, leaving their dirty dishes on the table, dashing toward the cafeteria exit.

Tara followed apprehensively, thinking they should be calling the police rather than chasing him down themselves. But she needn't have worried, since when the got to the doorway, the man was gone.

"Lobby," Max said urgently. "We'll catch him there."

They raced to the lobby but didn't see any sign of him. Not in the lobby, the surrounding area or in the visitor parking structure. Max's expression was darkly frustrated as they returned downstairs to the cafeteria.

"We were so close. We should have had him," he said.

"Maybe we should call Detective Graham?" she suggested. "Don't you think it's a little odd that he showed up here, the same day he shot at us?"

Max stopped and stared at her. "Yeah, actually I do. I can buy the fact he'd guessed where we'd taken Beau. I can see how he'd staked out the veterinary hospital waiting for us to return. But how on earth would he have known to come here to the hospital? It makes no sense that he'd be here."

"I suppose he could have followed us today," Tara said. "He's seen your rental car more than once. It might not be as far-fetched as we thought."

"Maybe." Max didn't sound convinced. "But he

would have had to follow us to the hotel first and then here. And even then, why would he just sit in the cafeteria? It's almost as if he's getting bolder or more reckless. Does he want us to see him?"

"I don't know." She bit her lip. "Steve Jasper might hold a grudge against me, but this does seem like odd behavior, even for him. The whole time we were following him, I tried to get a glimpse of his face, but I couldn't. I think he had brown hair, like Steve Jasper, but I can't even say that with one hundred percent certainty."

"Let's get out of here," Max said, taking her arm.

"What about Melissa?" Tara protested. She grabbed their trays and carried them to the tray line, glancing back at Max. "We came here to check on her."

"You're right," he relented. "It's not likely he can follow you inside the ICU."

"He's long gone from here I'm sure," she said reassuringly. "He might be trying to find new ways of taunting me, but he's not going to stick around to get caught."

"I still don't like it that he was here at all," Max grumbled as they headed toward the elevator.

She didn't, either—especially because once again her problems were interfering with his attempts to find Gary. She knew very well Max had stayed at the hotel as promised, just to keep an eye on her.

Max was tense, pacing the length of Melissa's room during their visit. She'd hoped he might pray with her, but he stood in the doorway, waiting for the nurse to come over.

"Hi, my name is Marietta. May I help you with something?" A young Hispanic woman asked.

"Are you my sister's nurse?" Max asked.

"Yes. I'm sure you'd like an update on her condition. Melissa has been stable most of the day. She had one episode of high intracranial pressures but that responded well to some medication. Doctor Kappel is pleased with her progress."

"Has anyone else been in to see her?" Max wanted to know.

Tara spun around to stare at him in surprise. Did he think her stalker would try to come up here? Or was he suddenly concerned that Gary/Garth/Billy might try to get in?

"No, there haven't been any other visitors," Marietta said, perplexed. "Only the two of you have been in to see her since her admission. Not counting the police officer who calls daily to see if she's woken up yet."

He clenched his jaw and nodded. "Okay, thanks."

"Max?" Tara crossed over to him. "What's wrong?"

"Nothing." He brushed off her concern, but she could still see something was bothering him. He turned and stared for a long moment at his sister. "Let's go. There's nothing more we can do for her here."

She didn't necessarily agree but wasn't sure what to make of Max in this new mood. She sensed arguing wasn't going to help. The nurse, Marietta, was already looking at them strangely.

"I'm ready when you are," she said.

Max was silent on the way back down to the main

lobby, but he remained alert, as if he were still on the lookout for her stalker.

"You know we're going to have to move into a new hotel," Max informed her.

"And you're upset about that?" She was still trying to figure out what was wrong. He seemed so angry, ever since they'd caught that glimpse of her stalker in the cafeteria.

"Yes, I'm upset. This guy is getting closer and closer to you, no matter what precautions I take. He almost killed you today." Bitterness laced his tone.

"You saved my life," she stressed.

"Yeah. But he followed us here, anyway. At the moment, I'm doing a lousy job of protecting you and a lousy job of finding Gary."

ELEVEN

And that was the crux of the matter, Tara guessed. Max wanted to be out tracking down Gary, instead of babysitting her. Not that his honorable soul would allow him to back off on trying to protect her. Especially after their close call outside the veterinary hospital.

Still, she didn't want to be his responsibility.

What could she say to make him feel better? He wouldn't leave her alone, even if she asked him to. And since her stalker had to have followed them to show up at the hospital, they did need to move to a new hotel.

For right now, all she could do was to try to make things as easy as possible for him.

An hour later, they'd packed their bags and had checked out of the hotel. She was surprised when Max flagged down a taxi.

"What about the rental car?" she asked, climbing into the taxi.

"I need to exchange it for a different one," Max said, his tone abrupt, as if he wasn't in the mood to talk.

She pinched the bridge of her nose and closed her eyes for a moment. Her stalker probably had recognized the car. Not only were they going to find a hotel farther away from the hospital but now he'd need to go through the hassle of trading his rental in for a new one.

All because of her.

"We shouldn't stay in a place far from the hospital," she tried to point out as the taxi sped away from the curb. "We need to be close. Melissa needs you."

"I know." He barely spared her a glance, leaning forward to talk to the taxi driver. "Take us to Thirty-fifth and Wallenbach Street," he instructed.

Thirty-fifth and Wallenbach? She had no idea where that was. East St. Louis, maybe, but it certainly didn't sound like they were heading for another hotel within a reasonable distance from the hospital.

Sure enough, when the taxi pulled over a good twenty minutes later, she realized what was at Thirty-fifth and Wallenbach.

Under the Beam.

The place was rather decrepit, peeling paint on the woodwork around the door frame, a side window with boards nailed over it. Worn brick lined the walls, and a broken neon sign hung above the door. From the outside, it looked like any other corner bar, although there was a small sign in the large picture window declaring they served food. The lights inside were dim, but through the one window not boarded up, she could see a few people seated at the bar.

"Wait here," Max said as he opened his door.

"I'll come with you," she said quickly, not at all comfortable with the idea of him going inside alone.

"This isn't your kind of place, Tara," he said impatiently. "Besides, there aren't many people inside. This won't take long, I'm sure."

"The meter's running," the taxi driver said.

"I know. I won't be long," Max repeated as he climbed from the car and slammed the door. He walked inside, and Tara sat huddled in the backseat of the taxi, peering through the window, tracking his progress.

True to his word, he was back in a few minutes, his facial expression grim. "No sign of Gary?" she asked.

"No. And no one claims to know him, either." His tone suggested he didn't believe they were being truthful. "The place isn't very busy, probably because it's a Sunday night. I'll come back tomorrow. Maybe I'll have better luck then."

"I'm scheduled to work tomorrow," she reminded him.

He cast a sideways glance. "I don't think that's a good idea. I'm sure your stalker knows to find you there."

She'd thought of that, too. "I can't take off indefinitely. My clients need me."

"Don't you have any vacation time?" Max asked. "Or maybe you can call in sick, at least for a couple of days. If Jasper is our guy, and he shows up at his parole office, the police will grab him. This could be all over for you by tomorrow afternoon."

She rubbed her aching temple. Calling in sick

wouldn't be right, since technically she wasn't ill. But considering her house blew up just two days ago, she was fairly sure her supervisor would grant her a personal day.

"One day," she agreed. "But I am going back to work on Tuesday, no matter what."

Max looked as if he wanted to argue, but he didn't. Smart man.

"Since we've decided I'm taking the day off tomorrow, I'm going to come back here with you. Maybe these guys will talk to a woman more easily than a man." A brilliant idea occurred to her. "I'll pretend I'm your sister, Melissa, explaining I need to talk to my boyfriend."

"No. Absolutely not." Max swiveled in his seat to stare at her incredulously. "Are you crazy? What if Gary's in there? He's going to know right away you're not Lissa. Besides, I already told you it's not your kind of place. I don't need your help on this, Tara. In fact, I refuse to allow it."

"Refuse?" There was nothing that got her riled up faster than being dictated to. "Now wait just a minute. I thought we were partners?"

"Not anymore," Max said with a note of finality. He leaned forward and gave the cabbie a new address, a hotel located not far from where they were originally staying.

Tara stared at Max, wondering what had happened. Wasn't it just yesterday at lunch that he'd told her how thankful he was that she was working with him to find Gary?

Clearly his feelings had changed.

She bit her lip and stared down at her hands. Or maybe the closeness she'd felt had been nothing more than her imagination.

Max sensed he'd hurt Tara's feelings, but there was no help for it. She'd be better off without him anyway. He was doing a lousy job of protecting her. He'd led her stalker straight to their hotel.

His ineptitude had nearly gotten Tara killed. More than once.

Checking into a new hotel, only a mile or so from the previous one, kept them preoccupied for a while. But once he was alone in a room across the hall from Tara, with no connecting rooms available this time, Max couldn't sleep.

His failures kept replaying over and over in his mind.

The night Keith died, it had been Max's idea to stay the night in the warehouse they'd staked out in Baghdad, when his buddy had wanted to return to their base camp instead.

He and Keith had been sent on a scouting mission to verify a tip they'd received regarding some Iraqi hostiles using an abandoned warehouse as a base of operations. They'd staked out the warehouse for over twenty-four hours, sweating through the hot afternoon sun and keeping watch over the long night. After the second day with still no activity, they'd decided to go in after darkness had fallen.

The warehouse was empty, and if it was being used as a base of operations before, it certainly didn't look it now. Keith wanted to head back, but Max had suggested they stay and sleep there for what was left of the night.

Keith had reluctantly agreed, and when he'd gone out to get the rest of their gear, he'd been ambushed. The hostiles had been on to them. Max had returned fire, hitting two of the insurgents and causing the rest to scatter before crawling over to where Keith was lying in the dirt, bleeding. His buddy had been seriously wounded.

Keith had died in his arms that night.

Because Max had failed him.

He ground the heels of his hands against his eyes, wishing he could erase the images seared into his brain just as easily. First Keith, then Lissa. Maybe he hadn't known his sister was in trouble, but wasn't that his fault, too? He'd been too preoccupied with his own issues to delve into what might really be going on with Lissa, here in St. Louis. He'd allowed their communication to skim across the surface, without getting down to the nitty-gritty details.

And now Tara.

He took a deep breath and let it out slowly. Three strikes and you're out.

He'd lost his faith in God, and one attempt at praying hadn't helped. And now, he'd lost his faith in himself.

Detective Graham called late the next morning, looking for Tara. Max walked across the hall and knocked on Tara's door, since the detective refused to talk to anyone except Tara herself.

"Yes?" Tara opened the door, looking at him expectantly, her exhausted gaze mirroring his lack of sleep.

"Detective Graham wants to talk to you." He glanced around the hotel hallway, not the best place for a conversation. "Maybe we should go down in the lobby, so we can both hear what's going on."

For a moment he thought she'd tell him it was none of his business, but she didn't. "I'll get my key."

They walked down to the lobby in silence. There was a small breakfast area off to the side with a few tables, so they chose one toward the back for some additional privacy.

Tara's fingers trembled a little when she dialed the detective's number. She kept the phone at an angle near her ear, silently inviting Max to lean close so he could listen, too. Her warm vanilla fragrance filled his senses.

The detective answered on the third ring. "Graham."

"This is Tara Carmichael," she said. "Max said you were looking for me?"

"Good news, Ms. Carmichael. Steve Jasper was apprehended today at the office of his parole officer. When we questioned him about you, he turned belligerent. Obviously the guy still harbors bad feelings toward you. And he has no alibi for any of the time frames in question, including Sunday afternoon's shooting outside the veterinary hospital."

The detective sounded hyped, satisfied that they'd gotten their man.

"Really? This is finally over?" Tara asked. "Is there anything I need to do?"

"Not yet. We're in the process of getting a search warrant for his apartment. We already have motive and no alibi, but it would be nice to have the attempted murder weapon, too. Or maybe something proving he'd made the bomb."

Max knew he should be relieved, but he couldn't help wondering why Jasper would bother showing up at his parole officer. Especially when Jasper had to know the cops would have an easy time finding him there. At the same time, it wasn't as if he'd tried to stay completely hidden, driving by the scene of Tara's house and following them to the hospital. He must have known they were on to him.

"Ask him what kind of weapon was used in the shooting," Max whispered to Tara.

Tara repeated his question.

"AK-47." Same kind of weapon used in the military. For some reason, the news bothered Max. "Like I said, once we search his apartment, I'm sure we'll have more to go on," Graham said.

"If you don't find anything at his apartment, will you have to let him go?" Tara asked.

"We've arrested Jasper and plan to hold him until his grand jury hearing. Since he has a record, I'm betting the judge won't let him out on bail. Don't worry. You're safe from this guy."

"Thanks," Tara murmured, relief evident in her tone. "Makes me feel better, knowing he's off the streets."

"Me, too. Take care, Ms. Carmichael. We'll be in touch."

Max straightened in his seat, gazing down at Tara. She was so beautiful, his chest ached. He tried to smile. "I'm glad they caught him."

"Me, too." Tara handed him his phone back. "I guess now I can focus on getting my house back."

He nodded grimly. Not an easy task, by any means. "Have you heard from your insurance company?" he asked.

"This morning. They agreed to make arrangements for me to stay at a cheaper hotel nearby while they repair my house. I guess the damage wasn't as bad as I assumed. They think it can be fixed."

He was surprised to hear it, since the repairs would be extensive, but then again, maybe that was better than demolishing the place and starting over. He was bothered more by the thought of Tara moving away to a different hotel. He'd gotten used to having her close by. "When do you leave?"

"Not until tomorrow." She glanced up at him. "Unless you want me to try to make arrangements to go immediately?"

"No," he hastened to assure her. "Tomorrow is plenty of time."

"Well, then." Tara rose to her feet. "I guess I'll head back to my room. The insurance company gave me a list of approved home repair companies. I have a few more yet to contact."

He almost offered to help but then realized he still

needed to find Gary. He'd told Tara they weren't partners anymore. And he'd meant it.

There was no sense in exposing her to more danger. No matter how much he liked being with her.

Early that evening, Max began to prepare for his return trip to Under the Beam. This time, he was taking a different approach.

He'd bypassed shaving, leaving his face scruffy. He went to the nearest Salvation Army store and found a threadbare fleece-lined flannel shirt, along with a pair of holey jeans and scuffed work boots. Best of all, he found a brown knit hat to hide his short military haircut.

With everything he'd found, he looked more like he was one of the regular customers. A guy who was down on his luck, who had nothing better to do than to hang out in corner bars on a regular basis.

He'd already discovered no one was going to talk to some uptight stranger asking questions about one of their own. And he suspected Gary was more comfortable in a place like Under the Beam than anywhere else. He didn't buy the idea that Gary had a lot of money. Unless he'd gotten his cash from illegal schemes. That was definitely believable. He wasn't sure why Lissa had kept the bar's matchbooks in her apartment, but he hoped to find out.

He'd go back several nights in a row, if that's what it took to track down Gary.

Parking his new rental car several blocks away, he trudged toward the bar, keeping his shoulders slouched and his head down. He was very glad he'd kept Tara far away from this joint.

He hadn't seen Tara since a few hours earlier, when they'd visited Lissa together. Tara had sat beside his sister's bed, praying, and while he'd watched, he was unable to join in.

The differences between them had never been clearer. She was in a class far above him. She didn't belong anywhere near the tavern he was soon going to make his second home. And it was too late for him to become a believer.

There were a lot more people in the place tonight, he noticed when he walked in. Probably because there was a Monday Night Football game on the small TV mounted in the corner.

Max squeezed onto a seat at the bar, keeping his head down as he ordered a club soda. He hoped no one would notice his lack of drinking, as he shrewdly scanned the patrons for any sign of Gary aka Billy.

Making himself comfortable, he pretended he had an interest in the game.

This was going to take a while.

Tara decided she really didn't like hotel rooms. They were too impersonal, too small, too confining.

Or maybe it was just that she'd spent too much time in this particular room.

Max had gone off without her. Even during their time together in Melissa's room, he'd seemed far away.

He hadn't prayed with her. He hadn't so much as

mentioned staying in touch once she left in the morning.

She was failing in her mission to save him.

What she needed was some sort of plan to get through to Max. Some way to get close to him again. It seemed that he was keeping her at arm's length ever since they'd caught sight of her stalker in the hospital cafeteria. She'd thought that after Jasper had been picked up by the police, things would get better between them.

If anything, the distance had gotten worse.

Maybe he'd grown tired of being with her. Of trying to protect her. She certainly couldn't blame him for that, since they'd been virtual strangers until a few days ago.

Circumstances had thrown them together. And now that those same circumstances had changed, they were free to go their separate ways.

Deeply troubled by the thought of not seeing Max anymore, she tried to think of a way to renew their friendship. A way to convince him to give Christianity a second chance. He'd attended the chapel service with her, had prayed for his sister, so he wasn't completely lost.

Although something had caused him to step back.

She thought back to the events that had taken place the day before. She and Max had been so close. He'd saved her life outside the veterinary hospital. That poignant moment outside her hotel room, when she'd thought he might kiss her.

And then seeing the guy in the blue baseball cap in the cafeteria. The wild chase to catch him, only to lose him.

Why had that caused Max to change?

Her cell phone rang, breaking into her thoughts. She glanced at the screen, but the display showed an unidentified number.

With a frown she answered. "Hello?"

"Is this Ms. Carmichael?" a male voice asked.

"Yes. Who's this?"

"This is Dr. Kappel from St. Louis General, and we've been trying to get a hold of Melissa's brother, Max Forrester, but he's not answering his phone. Your number is the only other number we have. Melissa's condition has taken a turn for the worse."

"Oh, no," she whispered.

"I'm afraid the news isn't good. You need to come in to see her. Before it's too late."

She gasped at the implication. "Are you saying she's going to die?"

"I'm saying I think you'd better hurry," he advised.

She didn't argue but hung up and tried Max's cell phone without success. He must have turned his phone off. She left a terse message about Melissa, hoping he'd check in before too long. Grabbing her purse and her jacket, she dashed down the stairs to the lobby.

Outside, she quickly made her way toward the hospital. This hotel happened to be on the north end of the building, the opposite end from the previous place, forcing her to take a roundabout path to the hospital. As she rounded the corner of the building, strong arms grabbed her from behind. One arm clamped around her chest. The other plastered a rag tightly over her nose and mouth.

"No!" Only a muffled sound reached her ears. Instinctively she bucked against her captor, using her feet to lash back at him and trying to twist out of his grasp, but he was too strong, his arm over her chest making it impossible to breathe.

She continued to struggle in earnest when he dragged her backward. Holding her breath and growing weaker with the effort, she tried to avoid the effects of the drug, desperately looking at the face of her captor. He lifted her up and stuffed her into the front seat of a black pickup truck, not completely letting go as he slid in beside her.

Gathering her strength, she lunged for the opposite door, but it was locked.

The cloth came away from her face, and she gasped for breath, but her relief was short-lived when he used his large body to practically sit on her, forcing her deep into the seat cushions. Then he completely covered her nose and mouth with the smelly rag.

She blinked, staring at him, not wanting to believe her struggles were useless. Despite the all-too-familiar navy blue jacket and cap, the deep scar running down the side of his face revealed his true identity.

Gary! The call about Melissa must have been a trap. He wanted to get her alone.

Her stalker was Gary!

TWELVE

Tara's lungs burned with the need to breathe. The rancid stench of Gary's sweat intermingled with the cloying sweet scent of the cloth made her want to gag. He was hurting her with his weight fully pressed against her. Yet his lopsided grin betrayed how he was enjoying every bruise he inflicted just a little too much.

She couldn't believe Gary was the one stalking her. Poor Steve Jasper was innocent. Red dots swam before her eyes as she continued to struggle against Gary's superior strength.

There was no way to escape him.

She closed her eyes and prayed. *Dear Lord, help me. Give me strength. Keep me safe.*

Her strength slowly seeped away, leaving her weak and trembling. Where was everyone? Where were the police? Hadn't anyone outside the hospital seen him grab her?

Where was Max?

Desperate with the need to breathe, she sucked air

into her oxygen-starved lungs. Instantly her vision blurred, and her surroundings faded away.

Praying to see God's light, she surrendered to the darkness.

Max pretended to watch the football game, even though the minutes dragged by like hours. The bartender was the same guy he'd talked to yesterday. He was the owner of the bar from what he surmised, so Max avoided him, seeking out someone else who might be a possible link to Gary.

The guy next to him pulled out a cigarette and asked for a lighter, but Max didn't have one.

So far, his undercover stint wasn't going so well.

At least the football game provided some entertainment. When one team fumbled the ball and the other team recovered, there was a loud unanimous groan from the patrons of the bar.

"When are those stupid guys gonna learn how to play?" the guy who'd asked for the lighter mumbled.

Max glanced over at him and took a chance. "No kidding." Max let out a snort of disgust, hoping to create a camaraderie that would help him ease into a conversation about Gary. He wasn't exactly sure what approach to take.

The lighter guy thumped him on the back. "Bunch of losers."

"You said it." Max frowned and glanced at his watch. "It's getting late. I'd have thought Gary woulda been here by now."

"Gary? You mean Scarface?" Lighter guy took a healthy slug of his beer. "Nope, I ain't seen him."

A thrill of excitement coursed through Max. Lighter guy knew Gary! Scarface couldn't be anyone else but Gary. Max wanted to pummel the lighter guy with questions but knew he had to proceed with caution.

He'd learned last night that the people who hung out in these sorts of places didn't appreciate questions. Especially about one of their own. One wrong move and the guy would clam up without telling him a thing.

"Hmm," Max grunted and took a sip of his drink. "Said he had a sweet deal for me. Told me to meet him here by eight. But it's nearly nine now."

"Don't worry. He'll show." Lighter guy pulled out another cigarette, lighting it with the book of matches the bartender had tossed at him. The same matchbook that he'd found in Lissa's purse and in her apartment. Max swallowed hard. He was convinced now that Gary had been here.

"He'd better show," Max grumbled, peering though the haze of smoke. "'Cause I'm in desperate need of some cash. I need that sweet deal he offered."

"Why don't you just call him?" Lighter guy seemed to be getting a little irritated with Max.

Max ducked his head, thinking of the cell phone he'd turned off and tucked deep into his pocket. How could he admit he didn't have Gary's number? He grimaced as if he were embarrassed. "I would, but somebody stole my phone."

Lighter guy muttered something crude under his

breath. He pulled out his cell phone and slid it across the bar at Max. "Here." His tone implied he should make the call and then shut up.

Max stared at the phone, anticipation shimmering through his veins. He opened lighter guy's phone and looked at the address book. Sure enough, Scarface had a local number programmed in.

Repeating the number over and over in his head, Max committed it to memory. Fingers tense, he dialed the number and listened to the ringing on the other end of the line, waiting for the moment he heard Gary's voice on the other end.

"Leave a message" was the brusque command. It was so brief, he couldn't even swear it was Gary's voice on the other end.

Dejected, Max declined to leave a message. He snapped the phone shut and handed it back to lighter guy. "No answer."

Lighter guy shrugged and slipped the phone back into his pocket, his attention centered on the game.

Max couldn't have cared less about the game. He continued to repeat Gary's number, waiting a good ten minutes before he headed off to the men's room. Inside the privacy of a bathroom stall, he quickly took out his phone and entered Gary's number for future reference.

Satisfied, he snapped his phone shut. Maybe he'd been too hard on himself. His undercover efforts hadn't been worthless after all. At least he'd gotten one clue. He could try calling Gary again, but identifying himself might give him away. It made more sense to turn the number over to the cop who was supposed to be work-ing on Lissa's case. Newton could probably dredge up an address for the guy. And once they had an address, they'd have Gary.

Things were definitely looking up.

His phone beeped, indicating he had a message. He frowned when he saw the call was from Tara.

"Max, Dr. Kappel has been trying to reach you. Melissa's condition has taken a turn for the worse. I'm heading over to the hospital to see her now. Please hurry."

Lissa was worse? His heart jumped into his throat as he stared at the message, realizing Tara's call had come in over an hour ago.

He needed to get to the hospital to see his sister.

Max shouldered his way through the crowd to get out of the bar. He broke into a run the minute he cleared the door.

Hoping and praying he wasn't too late.

Tara woke up slowly, biting back a moan as every muscle in her body throbbed with intense pain. She blinked and glanced around, realizing she was still in Gary's truck. Outside, the lights from the city were directly behind them. They were speeding down the highway, heading toward the river, going farther away from the hospital.

Her brain was still sluggish from whatever was in the cloth he'd pressed to her face. It took a few minutes to realize her hands were bound together at the wrists with something shiny. Duct tape? Her wrists hurt, and her fingers were already starting to go numb. She tugged against the bonds, but they didn't give an inch.

"So Sleeping Beauty is finally awake, huh?" Gary said with a sneer.

Tara swallowed hard and licked her dry lips. She would not let him see her fear. She counted her blessings. She was alive and he hadn't gagged her. "Where are you taking me?"

"Does it matter? It's not like you have a home to go to anymore, right?" He let out a bark of laughter at his own sick joke. "I have to say, watching your house explode was awesome. Huge points for the entertainment value, considering I only started following you because you interfered in my business."

"Your business?" She thought it would be best to keep him talking. Maybe if he was preoccupied she could find a way to escape.

There was no way to know when anyone would realize she was missing. Maybe her boss, if she didn't show up for work in the morning, although it was possible they'd assume she simply took another personal day. Max would get her message and try to find her.

"My business with Melissa. You drove her to that shelter, trying to get her to stop seeing me."

She was surprised. How on earth had he known? She hadn't put Gary on her list of suspected stalkers because Melissa had promised to keep Tara's identity a secret. "She told you?"

"She flaunted it in my face." His eyes turned cold. "Do you know how hard I had to work after that little stunt you pulled? Do you have any idea how much money I had to dump on her in order to get her to give me another chance? You're lucky to be alive after what you put me through."

Tara wasn't surprised at his revelation. Poor Melissa. She never should have allowed Gary back into her life.

"I hated you for that alone. Imagine my surprise when I saw you that next morning, outside your half-burned house, with none other than Max Forrester standing beside you. I knew at that moment my luck had changed."

"What do you mean?" His logic wasn't making much sense. He'd resented her for interfering with his and Melissa's relationship. What difference did it make that Max happened to be with her?

"You still haven't figured it out yet, have you?" His tone was full of disgust. In the dim lights, the expression on his face twisted with evil. "The only reason I targeted that stupid Melissa in the first place was to get back at Max Forrester for ruining my life."

Revenge. Tara's stomach sank to her knees. Gary had been motivated by nothing more than bitter revenge. Everything that had happened to Melissa had been nothing more than a way to get back at Max.

Payback. For arresting Gary and putting him in prison.

"Outside the veterinary hospital I had the perfect shot, so I took it. Your yappy dog made me miss. But seeing the way Max jumped in front of you, risking his hide to protect you gave me the idea."

What idea? She could only stare at him, too afraid to ask.

"You see, he obviously cared about you," Gary went on, seemingly enjoying filling her in on the gory details. "Maybe not as much as he cares about his stupid, brainless sister, but since Melissa was out of reach in the hospital I needed a new plan. Someone else to use as bait."

"Bait?" She couldn't help suppressing a shiver.

"Yeah. Bait." Gary stopped the truck at a red stoplight, leaning toward her with a leering grin. "You see, first I'm going to use you to get my hands on Max. Then I'm going to force him to watch as I kill you."

Tara sucked in a harsh breath, staring at him in horror.

Gary's eyes glittered with fevered hatred. "And then I'm going to torture him very slowly and painfully until he begs me to let him die."

Tara didn't want to hear any more of Gary's awful plans. There had to be a way out of here. Somehow, someway she needed to warn Max.

She couldn't let him walk blindly into Gary's evil trap.

But while she sought a way out, Gary continued to drive, heading farther out of the city, to an area near the water that she wasn't very familiar with. She tried to memorize the highway and street signs but lost track after he made several turns. Finally he turned onto a remote road, the truck bucking over the bumps in the road, until he reached a small, rustic log cabin.

"Home sweet home, baby doll," he drawled in that awful voice. "You can scream all you want. There isn't anybody within a fifty-mile radius who'll hear you."

Glancing around at the woodsy area, Tara was afraid he was right. She hadn't seen many signs of civilization over the past several miles. The gleaming water of the Mississippi River was only a hundred feet away, but there was no sign of a boat. Was she strong enough to swim across the river? It was worth a chance.

"Of course, if you annoy me, I'll be forced to punish you." Gary hopped out of the truck and swaggered around to her passenger door. "Get out," he snapped.

Awkwardly, unable to use her hands for leverage, Tara shimmied down from the truck, landing with a grunt in the dirt, nearly falling on her face but catching herself just in the nick of time.

Gary reached for her, but she shied away from his touch. Could she run for it? Swimming with her hands bound would be impossible, but she might be able to hide in the trees.

As if he'd read her thoughts, he grabbed her and tossed her over his shoulder, carrying her like a sack of potatoes into the cabin.

The interior was pitch-black. He threw her on the floor in the corner, and she couldn't suppress a cry of pain when her body landed with a thud and her head cracked against the wooden surface of the wall.

Closing her eyes she waited for the physical pain to

ease, listening as he moved about the cabin. Finally, he lit a lantern, providing some reassuring light.

Struggling to sit up, she leaned back against the wall, slowly inching upright, breathing hard with the effort.

The cabin was simple. Rustic. There was a fireplace against one wall and what looked to be a small bedroom off to the right. The kitchen was just as basic, with a two-burner stove next to a tiny refrigerator. A small wooden table and two chairs sat near the center of the room, in front of the fireplace. There wasn't any other furniture that she could see.

The place was messy, but from the discarded fast-food containers and the pile of wood near the fireplace, she thought it was possible Gary had been living here all this time while they'd been searching the city for him.

Gary tossed some wood into the fireplace and lit some of the kindling until he'd created a nice blaze of heat. Of course, she was in the corner farthest away from the blaze. Then he glanced over at her, his face drawn into a grotesque smile, since the muscles beneath the scar didn't move normally. Her stomach twisted when he slowly walked toward her, stopping mere inches from where she sat.

Give me strength, Lord, she prayed again, fearing the worst. *Please give me strength.*

"Here." Gary surprised her by thrusting a cell phone in her face. Her cell phone. He must have taken it when she'd been unconscious.

She stared at it blankly.

"Call him."

Max. He wanted her to call Max. When she made no move to take the phone with her bound hands, he pulled out a long, lethal-looking knife. The blade glinted sharply in the flickering light from the lantern. She shrank against the log cabin wall, but there was no place to go. He reached down and pressed the edge of the blade gently, but with clear intent, against her cheek.

"Call him," he repeated in a harsh tone. "Or I'll cut you until you look far worse than me."

Max rushed into the hospital, bypassing the elevator and taking the stairs two at a time until he reached the fourth-floor ICU. He wasn't breathing hard from exertion, but fear caused a cold sweat to dampen his skin.

Irritated at being slowed down by the woman seated behind the desk, he impatiently waited for her to unlock the door to let him in.

"Lissa," he said, rushing to his sister's bedside. He glanced up at the monitors, but it seemed like the numbers weren't much different than they had been earlier that day. He took his sister's limp hand in his. "Lissa, it's Max. I'm here for you."

He thought it was odd that there weren't a mass of doctors and nurses hovering at her bedside. He walked out into the hallway, glancing up and down the hallway but didn't see anyone sitting around. Several people were busy at other bedsides, obviously working hard.

Had they completely given up hope for his sister? Was Lissa's condition so bad they couldn't do anything more?

He went back inside to sit by Lissa. Surely they'd be in soon to talk to him.

And where was Tara? She'd told him she'd be here. Maybe she was down in the chapel praying.

Praying. He closed his eyes on a wave of overwhelming guilt. No matter what happened, he knew Tara believed in God's plan. In life after death. Life in heaven. Hadn't she told him to have faith? She was probably right now praying on his sister's behalf.

Praying. That's what he should have been doing, instead of going after Gary. What made him think he could play undercover cop? So he had Gary's phone number? What good would that do him if Lissa died?

No good at all.

Max sank into a chair next to his sister's bed, still clasping her hand tightly. Maybe this was his punishment for not believing in God. For not having enough faith. He'd grown up believing in heaven. But then watching Keith die, leaving a wife and children behind, and then seeing more of his men dying had made it difficult to believe. Now he knew that if Lissa was going to die he wanted her soul to be saved.

If it wasn't too late.

Humbled, he rested his forehead on Lissa's hand. "Forgive me, Lord. Forgive me for losing faith. For not believing. Please forgive Lissa, as well. She didn't mean to stray."

He hadn't meant to stray from the church, either. All

this time, he'd lashed out at God when really, he hadn't admitted his own guilt. As if he could have changed the outcome of Keith's death? If only he had realized God's will far surpassed his own.

Keith's death wasn't his fault. God had chosen to bring Keith to heaven. The way he had now chosen Lissa.

Finally a nurse came into the room, startling him from his prayers. "Hello, my name is Jennifer. I'm Melissa's nurse for the evening."

He scowled at her. Jennifer was far too cheerful considering the dire circumstances. "I got a phone call that Lissa's condition took a turn for the worse. What happened?"

Jennifer frowned. "Took a turn for the worse? No, not that I'm aware of. When was that? I started my shift at 7:00 p.m., and she's been doing fine since I arrived. In fact, Dr. Kappel's notes say he's planning to wean her from all the medications in the morning."

Perplexed, he stared at her. He hadn't misunderstood Tara's message. "But I don't understand." Suddenly his phone rang. Jennifer frowned at him when he glanced at the screen.

Tara.

"I'm sorry, but you can't use cell phones in here," Jennifer said. He ignored her. Something was wrong. Tara had left him a message about his sister being worse, but he belatedly realized he had no other missed calls from the hospital. A chill of apprehension snaked down his spine.

"Tara? What's going on? Where are you?"

"Hi, Max." Her voice sounded strange. "Gary wants me to say hello. Don't come," she suddenly said urgently, talking so fast the words ran together. "It's a trap! Don't come..." The last word was punctuated by a sharp scream.

The phone went dead.

THIRTEEN

Tara gasped. The sharp pain on her cheek where Gary had cut her with the knife had been far worse than she'd expected. Blinking away tears, Tara cowered in the corner, holding her bound hands over her burning cheek. A trail of blood dripped down her neck, soaking the collar of her sweater.

He ripped the phone from her hands, opened it and pressed the speed dial. "I have your little girlfriend here," Gary said to Max, having ripped the phone from her hands. "If you want her to live, you'll do exactly as I say. Understand?"

There was a pause as Max responded.

"Yeah, I thought so." Satisfaction surged in Gary's tone, and his face was pulled into that eerie lopsided smile. "Here's the deal. You're going to meet me. Alone. You get one chance. Don't mess it up. Because if I see anyone who even smells like a cop, I'll kill her."

Another pause.

"Don't hurt her?" Gary laughed maliciously. "Trust me, your sister's condition is going to look healthy compared to what I'll do to your girlfriend if you don't follow my orders. Don't even try to mess with me. I'll call you back in exactly one hour."

Tara pressed her eyes closed, wishing Max would just hang up on Gary. But she knew he wouldn't. He'd willingly risk his life for her. He'd done it before outside the veterinary hospital, hadn't he?

He'd come to her rescue. Even though he had to know Gary didn't plan on allowing either of them to survive.

Max was too honorable to walk away.

When Gary hung up her phone, he fiddled with the controls for a minute and then shut it off. Bracing herself for the worst, she looked up at him.

"Now I've got him," Gary gloated. He stuck her cell phone into his pocket and then began to pace the length of the small cabin. "He thinks he's so smart. *Lieutenant* Forrester? Thinks he can get promoted and arrest me? As if I did something wrong? I'm the one who's been scarred for life. What makes him so special? It's about time the *lieutenant* gets what he deserves."

Gary became more and more agitated, increasing his pace and mumbling unintelligibly. With the wall against her back, Tara pulled herself together. Her cheek didn't hurt that bad, but it was a prelude to something worse. She glanced around, seeking some way to escape. She wasn't just worried about herself. Somehow she had to prevent Max from giving up his life for hers.

The rustic cabin didn't offer a lot of options as far as

weapons to defend herself. The small wooden table and two chairs maybe, if she could lift them over her head. But not very practical. There weren't any fireplace tools, like a sharp poker or even an ax, near the woodpile. There might be utensils in the drawers someplace, but no doubt Gary would get to her before she found anything useful.

Turning her body slightly, to hide what she was doing, she smoothed her bound hands across the rough surface of the log-lined walls. Even a long splinter of wood would be better than nothing.

"He's going to pay for what he's done to me." Gary's voice dripped with fevered hatred. He still clutched the knife in his hand as he paced, the blade stained with her blood. "He's going to be sorry. I'm going to make him pay."

As she listened to his ramblings, she understood Gary's obsession was worse than she'd realized.

His thirst for revenge was insanely irrational.

Her fingers stumbled across something sticking out from between two logs. A nail? She didn't dare take her eyes from Gary but began to work on the nail, trying to wiggle it out from the log, even though there wasn't much more than a half inch protruding from the wood.

"He's going to watch while I hurt her. He's going to suffer. And when he begs me to let her live, I'll laugh in his face." Suddenly, Gary spun toward her. Her fingers froze on the nail, still partially imbedded in the wall.

She gasped when he thrust the knife in her face, the

tip of the blade pricking her skin. His foul breath made her gag. "You're going to die tonight. He's not going to beat me. Not this time. I hope you're prepared to die."

Instinctively, she shrank back against the wall, unable to tear her gaze from the threatening tip of the knife. She'd never been this close to instant death before. A metallic taste of fear coated her tongue. Gary's eyes were wild, his face twisted with hatred. She braced herself for another sharp swing of the knife.

Pure fear rushed over her, overwhelming her.

Her body trembled, and she couldn't breathe as she strained against the duct tape wrapped around her wrists. Tears of despair filled her eyes. He was going to cut her right now. Torture her. This couldn't be happening. She didn't want to die like this. She wasn't ready to die! There had to be a way to escape. There had to be.

Help me, Lord. Please save me.

She repeated the prayer over and over in her mind. Abruptly, a warm sense of calmness fell over her like a quilt, completely eliminating her frenzied panic. Instantly, her panic eased, leaving a wondrous sense of peace.

She had nothing to fear. God was with her. He loved her and cared about her. He'd never leave her. If she died this night, so be it. She'd be in God's hands.

No matter what Gary did to her, she was safe in the arms of her Lord.

Max clutched the phone, battling a wave of fury. Tara's scream reverberating through his mind. He didn't want to imagine what Gary was doing to her right now, but the images wouldn't stop parading through his brain.

That scream had been all too real. She was hurt. Badly. And it was all his fault. Somehow he must have led Gary to her. His stomach clenched and he bent over, trying to combat the pain.

If Tara died at Gary's hand, he'd never forgive himself. Never.

Blindly, he left Lissa's bedside and hurried down to the sparsely populated hospital lobby. He took several deep breaths, trying to calm down enough to think rationally. Rage wasn't going to help him rescue Tara. He didn't have much time. Gary was going to call back within the hour. He needed to pull himself together. He needed a plan.

No, he needed to call the police. Every nerve in his body resisted the idea, but he couldn't just walk into Gary's trap without any sort of backup. He couldn't handle this alone.

Tara's life was on the line.

He couldn't fail—again.

Gary's phone number was still in his cell phone. If he could get in touch with Newton, the cop working on Lissa's case, maybe they could use the number to track down Gary.

No, not Newton. He needed more power than a local cop. He needed to go straight up to Graham. The detective had seemed to care about Tara. Graham knew the background of their situation, and Max desperately needed the police on his side.

Graham wasn't happy to be bothered at ten o'clock at night on his personal cell phone. "What do you want now?"

"I need your help. Tara's been kidnapped."

"Kidnapped? What do you mean? We have Jasper in custody."

"Garth Williams, a former soldier in my army regiment, is the one who has her. He's using her as bait to get to me." And suddenly it was all crystal clear. Gary couldn't have found Tara by accident. There was no possible way Max could have led Gary to Tara.

But her stalker could have followed them. Her stalker had shown up at the hospital after that near miss at the veterinary hospital. Gary, or Billy, or whatever he called himself, had to be Tara's stalker. He must have targeted Tara because she'd helped Lissa. That's why none of the clues around Gary had made any sense.

The AK-47 was a weapon used in the army. Gary had shot at her outside the veterinary hospital. And when Max jumped in front of Tara, protecting her, he must have changed his plans. Max had wondered at the time why there had never been a second shot. Gary must have decided to kidnap Tara instead.

Gary hated Max. What better way to get back at him than to go after Tara? All of this was nothing more than petty revenge.

Tara had been targeted for revenge.

Now that he understood exactly how Gary and Tara's stalker all fit together, he quickly filled Graham in on the details of his new theory.

"I have Gary's cell-phone number," he told Graham. "It's a local number. Can you use it to get an address?"

"We can try," Graham admitted. "But he could have easily used a fake address. And don't even think about meeting him alone. We're going to be with you the whole time."

His fingers tightened on the phone. Gary's dire warning had been clear. Max needed to meet him alone. "No. I'm not wearing a wire, and you can't follow me too close. This guy has been in the military. He's likely scoped out the area. Possibly setting mine traps or trip wires for all we know. Besides, he's threatened to kill her if he smells a cop. I don't think it's an idle threat."

Graham was silent for a few seconds. "You said he's using Tara's cell phone to contact you? Cell phones have a locator function, so we should easily be able to pinpoint her location."

Graham was smart. The cell-phone angle just might work. "Meet me outside the hotel in fifteen minutes," Max advised grimly. "He's due to call me back in twenty."

Hanging up the phone, Max couldn't relax. He jogged across the hospital campus to their small hotel. He wanted to do more; he wanted to find Tara. He wanted to reassure her that he was coming for her and that he wouldn't let Gary kill her.

A rash promise, since there was always a chance he'd get there too late.

No. He couldn't be too late. If Gary wanted him to suffer, he'd surely keep Tara alive until Max got there.

He sank down on the bus-stop bench right outside the hotel, covering his face with his hands. Tara had to be okay. She just had to be.

Lord, please don't let Gary kill her. Take me instead. If I'm to die tonight, I'll gladly give my life for hers. Your will is my command.

He repeated the plea over and over in his mind. Suddenly, Max felt a strange sense of peace. Humbled, he realized he wasn't alone. He'd never been alone. Why hadn't he understood this before?

God was with him, always. He should have used God's help after Keith died, instead of pushing his faith away. Now, he needed to put the outcome of this night into the Lord's hands.

Gary called three minutes early. Luckily, it was mere seconds after Graham and his team arrived outside the hotel.

Max hushed them with a hand as he answered the phone. "I'm here, Gary. Where are you?"

"You're going to meet me at an abandoned barn located just south of Cannon Road a mile off Highway 3." Gary told him. "It will take you exactly twenty-five minutes to get there. The traffic is light at this time of the night. Don't be late or your girlfriend dies."

The phone went dead.

Max stared at Graham. "Did you get a location?"

Graham looked at the cop with the computer satellite screen. He shook his head with a resigned expression. "No. I was afraid of this. Your guy is smart. He must have the locator function turned off on Tara's phone. The closest we can do is pinpoint the source between the cell towers."

Max clenched his teeth, reining in his frustration. "Okay, so what sort of distance are we talking about? A mile? Two miles? Ten?"

"Roughly four square miles."

Four square miles? The equivalent of sixteen miles? Finding Tara in that wide span would be impossible.

Especially since Gary had him on a tight timeline.

"I have to go." Max strode toward his rental car. "You'll have to trust me."

"Wait," Graham said sharply. "We're coming with you."

Max glanced back, locking gazes with the detective. "No. Listen to me. Tara's life depends on you staying several miles behind me."

"You're not going in alone." Graham was firm.

"I'll keep my cell phone on, so you can use that locator function on me. When he calls me back, there's a distinct possibility he'll send me somewhere else, just to make sure I'm not followed. But you can trace my phone. That's the best we can do. Eventually, he'll lead me straight to where Tara is."

Graham nodded, understanding time was running out. They didn't have another option. "All right. Good luck."

Max spun on his heel and jumped into the rental car. He sped toward the highway, determined to get to the meeting place before Gary.

He'd made the distance in fifteen minutes, but Gary

wasn't anywhere around. And when his cell phone rang again, Max knew his instincts had been correct. Gary was going to send him on another path.

"Head south on Highway 3, go four and a half miles and turn left. Two more miles, you're going to turn right on a dirt road. Take it for ten miles. You'll see a driveway hidden beneath an overhang of trees. Turn there. If I don't see you on that dirt road in ten minutes, you can listen while I hurt her again."

Ten minutes. Max didn't hesitate but followed Gary's directions exactly. There was no time to call Graham with the new directions, but since Graham was going to triangulate on his cell phone anyway, it didn't matter.

Nothing mattered but getting to Tara.

He found the dirt road and had just cleared the trees when his phone rang again.

"You're lucky I can see your headlights," Gary said. Through the darkness, he could see the tall shadow of a figure silhouetted against the light in the cabin. Gary. His fingers tightened on the steering wheel. "That's right, come all the way up to the clearing. Get out of the car with your hands up, and come in through the front door."

Max did exactly as Gary instructed. Once he got out of the car, the silhouette vanished. After making sure his cell phone was on in his pocket, he raised his arms over his head. He approached the door, noticing it was partway open. He used his elbow to push the door aside.

He stopped abruptly, his heart dropping to the pit of his stomach when he saw them. Tara was huddled against the wall of the log cabin, sitting on the floor, her wide eyes surprisingly calm considering how Gary stood over her, his knife pressed against her throat.

Max tried to send her a reassuring glance, appalled at the cut on her cheek and the trail of blood dripping down her neck, staining her sweater. "Okay, I'm here now. You have me. You don't need her anymore. Let the woman go. This is between you and me, Billy. She's not a part of this." He purposefully used Gary's nickname, Billy, from when they were back in Iraq, hoping to rattle him.

Gary laughed. The uneven sound had an edge of insanity. "Oh, I don't think so. I have plans for her. And for you. Did you really think either one of you was going to leave here alive? I thought you were smarter than that, *Lieutenant*."

Max trusted Graham would get to the cabin soon. He needed to buy some time. Tara's safety was his first concern. He tried to think of a way to get Gary to leave Tara alone. What argument would work? He couldn't think of a single one.

"Don't be stupid, Max. I'm the one calling the shots here. Kick that door closed, and stand in the center of the room."

Max swallowed hard, unable to tear his gaze from the bloody scratch on Tara's cheek. The wound didn't look that deep, but the mark was hideous against her pale skin.

He kicked the door closed with his foot and stood in the center of the room, as directed. A quick glance around the interior revealed a table and two chairs as the only furniture. There was a fireplace against the far wall. And a small cabinet and two-burner stove in the kitchen area.

Nothing obvious to use as a weapon. There was no way to know how close Graham was to finding the cabin. Somehow he had to stall. Had to get Gary as far away from Tara as he could. "I didn't realize you were still such a coward, Billy. Anyone can overpower a woman. What's the matter? Are you afraid you can't take me?"

Tara's gaze widened in horror, and she shook her head, indicating she didn't want him to make Gary mad, egging him on.

Max ignored her.

The insult to Gary's ego worked. He lifted the knife away from Tara's skin, turning to face him, holding the knife at the ready, his eyes gleaming with the need to fight. "You think you're so strong? I can take you."

This was his chance. Max didn't wait another second. He bull-rushed Gary, hitting him hard and driving the former soldier back against the wall, as far away from Tara as he could manage.

Gary let out an angry yell as they went down. Max rolled on the cabin floor, away from Tara, bringing Gary with him. Gary's fighting skills weren't nearly as rusty as he'd hoped. They tangled on the floor for a moment, each trying to get the upper hand.

And then Gary twisted, bringing the blade of the knife slicing across Max's thigh.

Pain grabbed him by the throat. And for a split second, he relaxed his grip. Taking advantage of his lapse, Gary took control. He shoved Max backward and jumped to his feet, ready to attack again, only this time from a position of power. Max lunged upward to meet him, but before he could fully straighten upright, Gary's boot caught him square in the chest throwing him backward.

He couldn't keep his balance but slammed hard into the table and chairs, the wood table buckling beneath his weight. Max struggled to shove aside the broken timber, so he could get up and face Gary, even though the breath had been knocked from his body. He staggered to his feet, his back muscles spasming with pain, mingling with the burning sensation in his thigh.

Blood oozed from the stab wound, making the cabin floor slippery. He grabbed a hunk of wood from the broken table and held it out as a weapon. He might be injured, but at least with the chunk of lumber, the fight was a little more evenly matched.

Gary's face was drawn into a sneer, the knife ready in his hand as he approached. "You think you can take me? I'll prove which one of us is the better soldier. And you can bet it won't be you."

Max didn't answer, since it was clear Gary had forgotten all about Tara in his desperate need for revenge.

He was glad to be the center of Gary's attention. Max tossed a quick glance at Tara, trying to subtly signal her to go for the door. Her wrists were duct-taped together, but even so, there was no reason she couldn't get outside while Gary wasn't looking. Graham and the rest of the team would be here any minute.

This was Tara's chance to flee to safety.

FOURTEEN

Tara scrambled to her feet when Max faced Gary, clutching nothing more than a small length of wood that was clearly no match against Gary's lethal knife. She clutched the three-inch nail in her hand, trying to determine the best way to approach Gary.

Max was looking at her, his gaze exasperated, clearly indicating she should run for the door. She gave a sharp shake of her head. There was no way she was going to leave him.

Gary suddenly lunged at Max, lashing out with the knife, coming dangerously close to slicing his arm. Max belatedly jumped back, swinging the hunk of wood in Gary's direction, attempting to fend off the attack.

But Gary was quick and he spun around, with a judolike kick and hit Max's arm holding the hunk of wood. Max dropped his weapon but countered with a similar move, knocking Gary to the floor.

Only he slipped in the blood and fell, too. Gary lunged and lashed out with the knife, but Max caught his arm, stopping the knife mere inches from his face. Gary leaned all his weight onto Max, his face red with the effort to stab him, the two men locked in a deadly battle of strength and will.

This was the time to make her move. Tara grasped the nail in her tingling fingers, and she darted toward Gary. Max's eyes widened when he saw her, but she didn't hesitate, plunging the nail into the side of Gary's neck with as much force as her numb hands could muster.

Gary howled in pain, loosening his hold on Max. Tara scrambled out of the way. Max quickly gained the upper hand, as Gary reached for the nail protruding from his neck and yanked it out. Instantly, blood oozed from the wound. Max used the moment to his advantage, wrenching the knife from Gary's grip.

The cabin door burst open, and several men dressed in black SWAT-team gear rushed through the doorway. The police! Within seconds they'd surrounded Gary, who was still lying on the floor, pressing a hand against the wound in his neck. "Don't move. Garth Williams, you are under arrest for kidnapping and attempted murder."

Max stepped back from Gary, handing the knife to the closest SWAT-team member. "This is his weapon. He used it to cut Tara."

The cut on her cheek was minor compared to the cut on Max's thigh and the puncture wound in Gary's neck. She couldn't tear her eyes off Gary, who seemed to be losing blood at an alarming rate. Max was standing upright, hardly limping, but Gary was flat out on the floor. Had she hit his carotid artery?

She barely noticed as one officer took out another knife to cut through the bindings around her wrist. The returning circulation was painful, but Gary was clearly in worse shape. "You'd better call an ambulance. Gary needs medical attention."

"There's one on the way," Detective Graham assured, coming up beside her. He frowned when he saw the cut on her cheek. "Are you all right?"

"I'm fine. But Gary isn't." Guilt gnawed at her. She glanced around for something to stem the blood flow. "I need a rag or something."

"Here." Max pulled a hand towel out of a drawer in the small kitchen and tossed it to her.

Tara caught it and crossed over to Gary, kneeling beside him. "Move your hand. Let me take a look."

"Get away from me." Gary scowled and batted her hand away. "I don't need your help."

One of the SWAT-team members nudged Gary with the tip of his gun. "Don't touch her. Move your hand. We wouldn't want you to die before we have the chance to haul you to jail."

"Let me look," Tara said again softly, holding Gary's gaze with hers. "I need to apply pressure so you don't lose too much blood."

Gary stared at her for a long moment and then slid his gaze away in defeat, his hand falling away from the side of his neck. Tara peered down at the wound, deciding with her limited medical knowledge that she hadn't hit the artery, since the blood wasn't pulsating from the site. Breathing a prayer of thanks, she pressed the towel against the wound and applied gentle yet firm pressure to slow the bleeding.

She was conscious of Max watching her, as she rendered aid to the man who'd cut her and threatened to kill her. Tried to kill Max. When she glanced over her shoulder, she discovered he'd tied a similar towel around the wound in his thigh. She felt a little guilty over caring for Gary's wound instead of Max's, but he was staring at her, his gaze was full of admiration. Blushing a bit under his intense scrutiny, she looked back down to Gary.

The wail of sirens grew louder, indicating the ambulance had finally arrived.

She momentarily closed her eyes in relief. It was over. Melissa was safe. Max was safe. God had more than answered her prayers.

Thank you, Lord. Praise be to God.

Max had been forced to allow the paramedic team to provide care to the wound in his thigh, once they'd finished with Gary. Tara had hovered over him, gazing anxiously down at his wound. Luckily, it wasn't as deep as he'd originally thought. But the gash still needed stitches. He had to promise the paramedic team he'd go in to the hospital within the next few hours, before they'd allow him to decline an ambulance ride.

Graham came out of the cabin carrying an automatic weapon sheathed in a plastic bag, his expression filled with terse satisfaction. "We found this propped in the corner of his bedroom. How much do you want to bet the slug from outside the veterinary hospital is a direct match?"

Max summoned a smile. "I'm not a betting man, but I agree, I'm sure they'll match." He glanced around, looking for Tara. She'd disappeared when the paramedic began dressing his wound. The police had cordoned off the area around the cabin as a crime scene, and there were plenty of officers milling around, but he didn't see her. "Where's Tara?"

Graham frowned and turned to scan the area. "I thought I saw her a few minutes ago, heading around the cabin, to the riverbank."

The riverbank? Max gave a brief nod as he strode in that direction. The lights from the police cars behind them made it difficult to see, but as he grew closer to the riverbank, he could make out the silhouette of a slender figure seated on the ground.

"Tara?" he called softly, warning her of his approach. "Do you mind if I join you?"

Her arms were wrapped around her knees when she turned to look at him. "You should go to the hospital. I'm sure your leg wound needs to be sutured."

The distant note in her voice worried him. He sat down on the grassy riverbank beside her—close but not too close. "I'm fine. Tara, what's wrong? Why are you out here all alone?"

She was silent for a moment but then softly said, "I've never willingly hurt a human being before. I know I had to stop Gary, but I almost killed him."

He understood her guilt and shame. Hadn't he often felt the same way? "Tara, there's no need to worry. God has already forgiven you."

She made a soft sound and glanced toward him. Her face was pale in the moonlight, but he couldn't see the expression in her eyes. "You say that as if you believe it."

"I do believe it." He took a deep breath and glanced over at the rippling water of the Mississippi. "When I finally turned my phone on and listened to your message about Lissa, I ran to the hospital to see her. During those moments I thought for certain she was going to die, I realized how wrong it was to lose faith."

"Why did you?" she asked curiously. "Lose your faith, I mean?"

"During my college years, my father was very strict, and I guess I rebelled a bit. I wasted my time away from home, partying and generally not doing well in school."

"I'm sure lots of kids do the same thing."

She was being too nice, giving him far too much credit. He needed her to understand how far he'd fallen. "I grew distant from the church teachings I'd learned while growing up. I flunked out of school, and my dad tossed me out on my ear, telling me to figure out a way to support myself because he was finished with supporting me."

"Harsh," she murmured.

"Not really. Because I didn't have a lot of choices, I joined the army and soon learned there was a better way to live life than the way I'd chosen. After joining the army, I left my partying days behind me, embracing the chance to serve our country."

"So what happened then?"

He sighed and slowly shook his head. "I made a bad decision within the first few months after we'd been deployed to Iraq. My best friend, Keith, died. We weren't upset about being deployed to the Middle East. We were going to change the world. Instead, he died, leaving behind a wife and two small children."

"Oh, Max," Tara whispered, putting her hand on his arm. "That must have been awful. I'm so sorry."

"It was my decision to stay in that warehouse, and he was ambushed. The cost of my mistake was too high. I wrestled with guilt and lashed out at God, blaming Him. He was all-powerful, wasn't He? Surely He could have saved Keith if He had wanted to. I turned my back on Him then. And over the years, every time I lost another soldier, I piled more blame at God's feet." The realization shamed him now.

"I can see how hard that would have been for you, Max," Tara assured him. "But trust me on this. God is always there for you. I'm sure God understands the guilt you struggled with."

He couldn't help but smile. "Yes, that's just it. I believe very much in God's will now."

"You do?" Her tone was just a tiny bit skeptical. He couldn't necessarily blame her.

"Listen. As I was praying for Lissa, I received your phone call, trying to warn me about Gary. When you screamed, I nearly lost my mind. After I contacted the police, I prayed for God to spare you. I prayed for him to take me instead. And suddenly, I can't really explain how, but I knew He was with me. The panic and fear were overwhelming, but suddenly I was filled with a strange sense of peace. And I realized that God had never abandoned me and that he never would as long as I was true to Him. As long as I believed."

Her fingers tightened on his arm, and he wished he could see her face more clearly.

"I guess that sounds a little hokey to you, huh?" he asked, embarrassed.

"No, Max. That doesn't sound hokey to me at all," she admitted in a husky voice. "In fact, I'm so happy to hear you say that. Becoming a true believer is the path to eternity. And you should know that I had a very similar experience here, when Gary was threatening me with the knife. For a moment I was so afraid of dying, until God reminded me that he was always with me."

He hated thinking of how close she'd been to being seriously hurt. Wrapping an arm around her shoulders, he hugged her close. "I'm so glad you're all right, Tara," he murmured. "I was so angry when I had captured Gary's full attention, but you didn't take the chance to run and save yourself."

To his surprise, Tara slid her arm around his waist and hugged him back. His heart swelled with love. True, light-blinding love. Tara wasn't anything at all like Clare. She was stronger—emotionally and spiritually— than Clare had ever been.

"I couldn't leave you, Max," she said simply. "I didn't want you to die."

He reached up and smoothed the loose strands of hair, which had come undone from her braid, away from her face, gently avoiding the cut on her cheek. "Tara, I've never met anyone like you," he admitted. "You are truly a very special woman."

She stared up at him, her expression solemn. "I think you're pretty special, yourself, Lieutenant Max Forrester."

Her admission shot a spear of hope to his heart. Was it possible that this time he wasn't mistaking gratitude for something more? Could it be that Tara cared about him as deeply as he cared for her?

He'd never felt closer to another human being as he did right at this moment.

Hesitantly, giving her plenty of time to draw away, he lowered his mouth to hers in a soft kiss.

Reveling in the sweet way she returned his kiss.

Tara regretfully broke off Max's kiss, burying her face against his chest, thankful for the darkness surrounding them so he couldn't see her fiercely red cheeks.

What was she doing? How could she kiss Max like this? How on earth could she forget about Ted, the man she'd promised to love forever?

Max had saved her life. And she'd helped save his, too. There would always be a special bond between them after the events that had transpired this night. But she couldn't be in love with him.

She refused to allow herself to be in love with him.

Pushing herself away from the warmth of his chest, she averted her gaze. The damp earth beneath her caused a chill. "I think we'd better go. You need to get to the hospital. Deep cuts like yours need to be taken care of quickly."

"I suppose you're right." Max reluctantly dropped his arms. He stood, letting out a low groan when he placed his full weight on his injured leg. He reached out to take her hand, helping to lever her to her feet. "I'll drop you off at the hotel first. I'm sure you want to get cleaned up."

"Hospital first," she said firmly. No matter how badly her feelings were tangled up over Max, she couldn't bear to let him go to the hospital alone. No doubt he'd need a strong course of antibiotics to ward off infection.

He frowned a bit, staring down at her and brushing a finger lightly along the cut on her cheek. "Maybe you're right. You should come with me. I think someone should take a close look at this cut of yours, too."

She knew the cut wasn't deep but didn't bother to correct his assumption. If he wanted to think she was coming along to have her scratch looked at, then fine. At least he'd get the attention he needed to the wound on his leg.

When Max took her hand in his, she found she was glad for his touch, even though she knew she shouldn't be. Was it so wrong to take comfort in his company, after everything they'd gone through? Surely they'd grown close, partners in defeating Gary's attempt to harm them.

All too soon, the Thanksgiving holiday would come and go, and Max would be on a plane returning to Iraq to fulfill what remained of his tour of duty. Hopefully, his sister, Melissa, would continue her road to recovery. For all she knew, Max was determined to sign up for another tour of duty, now that he'd accepted God as his savior.

She was pleased for him. Thrilled that he'd accepted the Lord. Although she hadn't really had much to do with saving him, she was at peace with the mission God had set out for her. There would always be another soul to save.

And she had the daunting task of rebuilding her home looming before her. Between her work and rebuilding her home, she wouldn't have time for anything else.

"I'll drive," she offered as they made their way around the cabin to where Max's car was standing on the gravel driveway. He'd begun to limp, just a little, favoring his injured leg. The police had begun to disperse from the scene, as well. The rustic cabin had so much potential. It was too bad Gary had taken something beautiful and turned it into something awful.

"I'm fine," he insisted. She rolled her eyes at his macho attitude. "The injury is in my left leg, not my driving foot."

She suppressed a sigh, sliding into the passenger seat without complaint. Max backed out of the driveway and onto the road. The interior of the car was silent but comfortably so. Almost as if words between them weren't necessary.

As she watched the lights of the city grow brighter, she knew that after tonight there wouldn't be a reason to spend more time with Max. He didn't need to be her mission anymore. Maybe they could go to the hospital together to visit Melissa to make sure she was really doing all right.

But then she'd go her way, and he'd go his.

Her chest tightened. The scenery outside her passenger window became nothing more than a hazy blur. The very thought of giving up Max's companionship left her feeling horribly bereft.

FIFTEEN

Max waited for hours in the St. Louis General Hospital E.R. to be treated. When they finally took him back into a room, he'd insisted they look at Tara's cheek first. Which made the nurse sigh in annoyance, because that meant she had to get them both registered in the computer. The nurse warned him that he'd have to wait longer.

With Tara seated at his side, it was difficult to care about the delay.

His heart was so full of love that he thought it might burst. Yet he wasn't in a position to broach the topic of the future with Tara. Lissa still needed him. Even though Gary was safely in jail, he wanted to make sure Lissa was really on the road to recovery. Thanksgiving was only a week away, and two days after that, he was scheduled to hop a flight back to Germany and then on to Iraq.

There were only a few months left of his tour of duty. Even if he didn't reenlist with the army, what would he do once his four-year stint was up? He needed to find a steady job with benefits, which could be a challenge considering the dismal state of the economy. Without some sort of future planned, he had nothing to offer Tara.

Nothing but his love.

Which he couldn't be one hundred percent sure she'd accept and return.

Tara had risked her life for him. From the moment they'd met, their lives had been intertwined in a tailspin of danger. Now that the threat had passed, they needed time to get to know each other. He wanted to talk to her, to know everything about her, but not here. Not in the busy E.R. with people constantly milling around, interrupting them.

Besides, Tara needed some time to decompress after her ordeal. He still couldn't believe how she'd leaped up and stabbed a nail into Gary. He could only imagine how traumatized she must feel.

"I hope you're still not planning to go back to work tomorrow," he said, once the nurse had finished thoroughly cleaning out his wound.

Tara blinked and he realized she was curled up in the chair, half-asleep. "What time is it?"

"Two-fifteen in the morning." He wished she'd have gone back to their hotel but didn't want her walking through the night alone. She'd explained about the fake phone call and how Gary had grabbed her while she'd been walking from the hotel to the hospital to check on Lissa.

"That late?" She lightly fingered the dressing on her

cheek. The nurses had washed her face and had called in a plastic surgeon to look at the cut. He'd claimed it wasn't too deep and had applied a series of butterfly bandages over the worst of it, reassuring her that the mark wouldn't likely leave a scar.

"Yes. That late. Too late for you to even think about going in to work tomorrow."

"I doubt if I will." She hid a yawn behind her hand. "I can take another personal day, as long as my boss doesn't get angry with me."

She'd been kidnapped, her life threatened and she thought her boss might get angry? "I'll talk to him. I'm sure he'll understand."

Tara chuckled softly. "My boss isn't a he, she's a she. Thanks for the offer, but I can handle this one myself. Besides, it's not just that I'm taking another personal day. It's knowing that with everything I have to do to rebuild my house, this is likely the first of many days I'll need off."

It was on the tip of his tongue to offer his help, until he remembered he wouldn't be in St. Louis for much longer. "I can help in the time I have left. You don't have to handle everything alone."

She didn't pounce on his offer like he'd expected. "Let's wait to see how Melissa does first, okay?"

He didn't have time to respond since the doctor chose that moment to come into the room, suture tray in hand.

Bracing himself for the pain, reminding himself that he'd been through much worse over the years, he was surprised when Tara took his hand, wordlessly offering support and a hint of comfort.

Getting sliced with a knife wasn't so bad. He'd endure far worse with Tara sitting beside him, holding on to his hand.

Tara awoke late the next morning, blinking at the generic surroundings of her hotel room, her entire body stiff and sore. There were faint bruises encircling her wrists, but other than the cut on her face, she was fine. Max was safe. Gary was in jail. All in all, she had nothing to complain about.

Time to begin putting the pieces of her life back together.

After a quick shower, she called the St. Louis Police Department so she could get in touch with Detective Graham. Physically, she was safe now that Gary was in custody, but she still needed to get to the bottom of her emancipated checking account.

Detective Graham admitted he'd forgotten about that detail and promised to call her back in a few minutes. She braided her hair while she waited, hesitating for a moment as she wondered what Max would think if he saw her with her hair down.

Ridiculous to think such frivolous thoughts when she had so many more important things to worry about. Rolling her eyes at her own foolishness, she continued braiding her hair, determined to keep her relationship with Max in its proper perspective.

When Detective Graham called her back, he had

good news. Gary had, indeed, gotten her bank account information when he'd been inside her house. Apparently he had a hacker friend who'd moved everything out of her account into a new account in his name. Luckily, Gary hadn't spent much of the money, and Detective Graham promised whatever was left would be returned to her. Plus they'd force Gary to sell his property to make up any difference.

What a relief to know she wasn't as broke as she'd originally feared. Although after she paid for the repairs on her car and reimbursed Max for everything he'd done for her over the past several days, there would still be a serious dent in the amount she normally needed for living expenses.

She chewed her lower lip thoughtfully. Maybe the mortgage rates had dropped again. If so, she could refinance her house again to lower her payments.

No, that wouldn't work. What was she thinking? She couldn't refinance a partially burned house.

A cheaper hotel would help. Especially since her insurance company was willing to pay for the bill. She began packing up her meager belongings, thinking of the best way to get across town to the hotel located closer to her home. The bus was probably her best option.

A knock at her door made her jump, knocking her bag to the floor. "Tara? Are you in there? Open up. It's Max."

Max? Here she'd been trying so hard to push him out of her mind, yet he'd come to find her. Was something wrong? She hurried over to the door. "Hi. What's going on?"

He didn't look distressed; in fact, his eyes were blazing with excitement, a wide grin splitting his face. "The hospital just called. Lissa's awake! She's asking to see me."

Thank You, Lord. Her heart swelled with joy, and she smiled, truly happy for him. "Max, that's wonderful news."

"What are you waiting for?" he asked impatiently when she didn't move. "Come on, let's go."

She hesitated, then grabbed her purse and followed him down the hall to the lobby. Melissa was her client. There was nothing wrong with wanting to see, with her own eyes, that she was really all right.

"Lissa's waking up is nothing short of a miracle," Max was saying, as they crossed the hospital grounds. "I didn't deserve it, but God still granted me a miracle."

"A true miracle," she agreed, privately thinking he did deserve it. He served his country and had put his life in jeopardy to save her. "Do you think we should tell her about Gary?"

Max's lips thinned. "Only that he's been arrested and will be in jail for a long time. The slight detail about how he was using her to get to me can wait until later."

"I understand. She'll have enough to deal with as it is. She needs to focus on getting healthy, nothing more."

Max nodded. Within minutes, they were upstairs in the fourth-floor ICU. "Lissa?" Max asked hesitantly, as he entered her room.

Melissa turned her head toward Max. The breathing tube was gone, and the bruises were fading, but the fearful expression in her eyes still lingered. Her lower lip trembled, as if she were about to cry. "I'm sorry, Max. I didn't mean for this to happen. I ruined your Thanksgiving homecoming. I'm so sorry."

"Shhh, don't worry about a thing. None of this is your fault, do you hear me? None of it." He crossed over to the bed and leaned over, pressing a kiss to her forehead and taking her hand in his. "I love you, Lissa. I'm so glad you're doing better. Nothing else is important right now. Although you should know that Gary's in jail. He's never going to hurt you or anyone else, ever again."

"Jail?" Her eyes widened. "How? When?"

"It's a long story. I'll fill you in on all the details later."

"Good. I'm glad he's in jail. He hurt me." Melissa's eyes filled with tears, and Max wrapped her in a consoling hug, murmuring reassurances.

Tara watched the two of them, her own eyes smarting with tears. As much as she cared about both of them, her presence wasn't needed here. In fact, she was intruding on what was obviously a private moment between brother and sister.

Tara took a few steps backward until she could ease away, leaving them alone in the room.

Days later, Tara sat on the bank of the river, next to Gary's abandoned cabin, as Beau sniffed the base of every tree. The crime-scene tape had been taken down, and now the place seemed broken-down and lonely. In spite of everything that had happened there, she found sitting on the bank, watching the rippling water of the Mississippi River flow past, extremely comforting.

She hadn't seen Max in almost a week. He'd called her several times, but she'd put him off, explaining she was too busy with work and dealing with her house to make time to see him. But that wasn't entirely the truth.

She wanted to see Max. She missed him. Terribly.

The knowledge was troubling.

She'd come here, after church on this Sunday afternoon, to try and sort out her feelings. Gazing at the mesmerizing water, she forced herself to be honest.

In those moments, when Gary was on the verge of killing Max, her heart had squeezed painfully in her chest. She'd been willing to attack Gary, acting completely out of character, to save Max's life.

And afterward, when she'd realized Max had accepted the Lord as his savior, she'd known how much she cared for him.

How much she loved him.

She sucked in a harsh breath and closed her eyes. How could this be possible? She'd loved and married Ted. She and Ted had known each other for years, having grown up attending the same church together. He'd only been gone eighteen months.

She'd just met Max. And under extreme circumstances, too. Surely these troubling feelings she had for him weren't real.

But if that were the case, why did she long to be with him?

Help me, Lord. Give me guidance. Help me to understand what you want of me. Help me to understand my feelings. Help me so I don't betray Ted.

"Tara?" Her name spoken in the all too familiar deep voice interrupted her prayer and made her twist around. "What are you doing out here?"

Max. Instantly her heart soared. He looked wonderful. So tall, so strong. In that moment, the sun broke through the clouds, illuminating the area around them in warm sunlight.

The poignant moment made her catch her breath. Love could never be a betrayal. How could she have been so blind? God's love was overwhelming and all-encompassing. Loving Max didn't change her feelings for Ted. Her love for Ted had prepared her in loving Max.

The abrupt realization clogged her throat so she could barely speak. "I could ask you the same question," she said, her voice husky. Beau rushed over to Max, his tail wagging.

Max bent down to scratch the dog between his ears, then straightened, his gaze guarded. "I came out here for the same reason you did, I expect. To escape the noise of the city. Seeking a little peace and quiet."

"Yes." She was amazed he understood and felt the same way. But she wasn't sure what his feelings were toward her. He'd kissed her, but for some men that didn't mean much. She turned back toward the water. "It sure is beautiful out here."

"I'm glad you aren't bothered by the memories of what happened here."

She slowly shook her head.

Max was quiet for a moment and then came up beside her. "Tara, do you mind if I ask why you've been avoiding me?"

The flash of hurt in his eyes made her feel guilty. "I'm sorry, Max. I didn't mean to avoid you. I've been...confused, I guess."

"Confused?" He dropped down onto the ground beside her. Beau tried to jump into his lap then dashed off to chase a squirrel. "About what?"

She ducked her head, embarrassed. Baring her heart wasn't easy, but he deserved to know the truth. "About you. I care about you, Max. A lot."

"You don't sound very happy about it," he said dryly. "Tara, why is that such a bad thing? You must know I care about you, too. I've been miserable this past week without you." He took her face in his hand and forced her to meet his gaze. "Tara, I love you."

"Really?" She couldn't completely hide the doubt in her tone. She and Ted had known each other for years. How could she trust Max's feelings were the same as hers?

"Yes. Really. I love you, Tara, even though I know I don't have much to offer," Max said slowly. "And asking you to wait for me is asking a lot. But maybe when I return home in a few months, you wouldn't mind if I called you? Then we could get to know each other again, under more normal circumstances."

"I would like that," she admitted. But then, realizing she was being a coward, she decided to tell Max the truth. "But time and normal circumstance aren't going to change how I feel about you, Max. I love you. With my whole heart and soul. I'm more than willing to wait for you, for as long as it takes. You have everything to offer me, because your love is all I want or need."

The muscles of his arms bunched under her fingers as his entire body tensed. "Are you sure? I'll understand if you need time. I don't want to rush you."

"I'm sure." And she was. How could she have doubted God's plan right from the start? He'd put Max in her life not just to be her mission but also to give her someone to love.

"Tara," he murmured, pulling her into his arms, for a sweet kiss. "I'm so lucky to have found you."

She smiled up at him. "Luck didn't have anything to do with it. God brought us together, Max."

"You're right. He did. And I'm eternally grateful." Max gently kissed her again, and this time, she opened her heart to his. When he broke off the kiss, leaving her breathless, he suddenly jumped to his feet, bringing her upright, too. "Come on. We have to tell Lissa."

"We do?" Laughing, she followed him toward their cars. Beau quickly joined them.

"Yes." He stopped suddenly, turning toward her, his face serious. "Will you share Thanksgiving with us? Lissa's being discharged from the hospital in a few days, and I promised to cook dinner to celebrate."

She would love nothing more than to be with him over the holiday, but still, she hesitated. "I'm not so sure how Melissa will feel about that. Maybe you and your sister should spend the holiday alone, the way you originally intended to. I can wait."

"But I can't. Tara, it was Lissa's idea to invite you. Besides, you're part of my family now. You and Beau. Starting today and lasting forever."

Forever. She loved the sound of that.

* * * * *

Dear Reader,

God bless the brave military men and women who dedicate their lives to protecting our country!

In my first Love Inspired Suspense book, you will meet Lieutenant Max Forrester, on leave from Iraq and anxious to spend Thanksgiving with his sister, only to find she is clinging to life in the ICU after a brutal attack by her boyfriend. His path intersects with social worker Tara Carmichael, who is still grieving for her dead husband. The moment Tara and Max meet, their lives are irrevocably entwined together.

As Max searches for the man who had hurt his sister, he discovers Tara's life is in danger from a mysterious stalker, Tara soon realizes her mission is to help Max rediscover his faith and eagerly accepts the challenge, but neither of them is entirely prepared for the danger lurking right around the corner. Only after they embrace God's love will they be free to love each other.

I hope you enjoy reading *The Thanksgiving Target*.
Yours in faith,
Laura Scott

QUESTIONS FOR DISCUSSION

1. In the beginning of the story, Tara feels guilty for not doing more to protect Melissa Forrester from her abusive boyfriend. Do you think her guilt is misplaced, or could she have done more?

2. Tara has reached out to Melissa. Are there people in your life who you could reach out to in love and faith?

3. Despite Tara's faith in God, she is struggling to accept the loss of her husband. Have you lost a loved one, and how have you used your faith to overcome your grief?

4. Max has turned his back on his faith, especially after losing his best friend in Iraq. What is the turning point that leads him to the path of the Lord?

5. Tara doesn't understand her purpose in life or the mission God has for her. Identify your mission in life, and share with the group.

6. Max agrees to attend a church service with Tara, but he doesn't really participate. Have you held back from being more involved in your church community, and if so, why?

7. Max decides he's not good enough for Tara because he's lost his faith. Discuss if this is his way of being noble or taking the easy way out.

8. When Tara is kidnapped, she panics, allowing fear to overcome her faith. Has this ever happened to you? If so, explain.

9. During Tara's darkest hour of despair, she feels God's presence and is filled with peace. Describe the situation in which you have felt closest to the Lord.

10. Max uses his renewed faith to help him find Tara, who is being held in the rustic cabin on the Mississippi River. Have you ever experienced a similar revelation? If so, explain.

11. Tara and Max believe their prayers and their faith in God have helped to heal Melissa. When have you experienced a similar miracle in your life?

12. Thanksgiving is a special holiday, a time to rejoice in God's love and to thank Him for all our blessings. Which blessings are you most thankful for?

Here's a sneak peek at "Merry Mayhem" by
Margaret Daley,
one of the two riveting suspense stories in the new
collection CHRISTMAS PERIL, available in
December 2009 from Love Inspired Suspense.

"Run. Disappear… Don't trust anyone, especially the police."

Annie Coleman almost dropped the phone at her ex-boyfriend's words, but she couldn't. She had to keep it together for her daughter. Jayden played nearby, oblivious to the sheer terror Annie was feeling at hearing Bryan's gasped warning.

"Thought you could get away," a gruff voice she didn't recognize said between punches. "You haven't finished telling me what I need to know."

Annie panicked. What was going on? What was happening to Bryan on the other end? Confusion gripped her in a chokehold, her chest tightening with each inhalation.

"I don't want—" Bryan's rattling gasp punctuated the brief silence "—any money. Just let me go. I'll forget everything."

"I'm not worried about you telling a soul." The menace in the assailant's tone underscored his deadly intent. "All I need to know is exactly where you hid it. If you tell me now, it will be a lot less painful."

"I can't—" Agony laced each word.

"What's that? A phone?" the man screamed.

The sounds of a struggle then a gunshot blasted her eardrum. Curses roared through the connection.

Fear paralyzed Annie in the middle of her kitchen. Was Bryan shot? Dead?

The voice on the phone returned. "Who's this? Who are you?"

The assailant's voice so clear on the phone panicked her. She slammed it down onto its cradle as though that action could sever the memories from her mind. But nothing would. Had she heard her daughter's father being killed? What information did Bryan have? Did that man know her name? Question after question bombarded her from all sides, but inertia held her still.

The ringing of the phone jarred her out of her trance. Her gaze zoomed in on the lighted panel on the receiver and saw the call was from Bryan's cell. The assailant had her home telephone number. He could discover where she lived. He knew what she'd heard.

"Mommy, what's wrong?"

Looking up at Jayden, Annie schooled her features into what she hoped was a calm expression while her stomach reeled. "You know, I've been thinking, honey, we need to take a vacation. It's time for us to have an adventure. Let's see how fast you can pack." Although she tried to make it sound like a game, her voice quavered, and Annie curled her trembling hands until her fingernails dug into her palms.

At the door, her daughter paused, cocking her head. "When will we be coming back?"

The question hung in the air, and Annie wondered if they'd ever be able to come back at all.

Follow Annie and Jayden as they flee to Christmas, Oklahoma, and hide from a killer—with a little help from a small-town police officer.

Look for CHRISTMAS PERIL by Margaret Daley and Debby Giusti, available December 2009 from Love Inspired Suspense.

REQUEST YOUR FREE BOOKS!
2 FREE RIVETING INSPIRATIONAL NOVELS
PLUS 2 FREE MYSTERY GIFTS

Love Inspired®
SUSPENSE

YES! Please send me 2 FREE Love Inspired® Suspense novels and my 2 FREE mystery gifts (gifts are worth about $10). After receiving them, if I don't wish to receive any more books, I can return the shipping statement marked "cancel". If I don't cancel, I will receive 4 brand-new novels every month and be billed just $4.24 per book in the U.S. or $4.74 per book in Canada. That's a savings of over 20% off the cover price. It's quite a bargain! Shipping and handling is just 50¢ per book.* I understand that accepting the 2 free books and gifts places me under no obligation to buy anything. I can always return a shipment and cancel at any time. Even if I never buy another book, the two free books and gifts are mine to keep forever.

123 IDN EYM2 323 IDN EYNE

Name	(PLEASE PRINT)	
Address		Apt. #
City	State/Prov.	Zip/Postal Code

Signature (if under 18, a parent or guardian must sign)

Mail to Steeple Hill Reader Service:
IN U.S.A.: P.O. Box 1867, Buffalo, NY 14240-1867
IN CANADA: P.O. Box 609, Fort Erie, Ontario L2A 5X3
Not valid to current subscribers of Love Inspired Suspense books.

Want to try two free books from another series?
Call 1-800-873-8635 or visit www.morefreebooks.com

* Terms and prices subject to change without notice. Prices do not include applicable taxes. Sales tax applicable in N.Y. Canadian residents will be charged applicable provincial taxes and GST. Offer not valid in Quebec. This offer is limited to one order per household. All orders subject to approval. Credit or debit balances in a customer's account(s) may be offset by any other outstanding balance owed by or to the customer. Please allow 4 to 6 weeks for delivery. Offer available while quantities last.

LISUS09

Love Inspired®
SUSPENSE

TITLES AVAILABLE NEXT MONTH
Available December 8, 2009

CHRISTMAS PERIL by Margaret Daley and Debby Giusti
Together in one collection come two suspenseful holiday
stories. In "Merry Mayhem," police chief Caleb Jackson
is suspicious when a single mother flees with her child to
Christmas, Oklahoma, where danger soon follows them. In
"Yule Die," a medical researcher discovers her patient is her
long-lost brother—with a determined cop on his tail.

FIELD OF DANGER by Ramona Richards
Deep in a Tennessee cornfield, April Presley witnesses a
grisly murder. Yet she can't identify the killer. Until the
victim's son, sheriff's deputy Daniel Rivers, walks her
through her memory—and into a whole new field of danger....

CLANDESTINE COVER-UP by Pamela Tracy
You're not wanted. The graffiti on her door tells
Tamara Jacoby someone wants her out of town.
Vince Frenci, the handsome contractor she hired to
renovate the place, wants to protect her. But soon they
discover that nothing is as it seems...not even the culprit
behind the attacks.

YULETIDE PROTECTOR by Lisa Mondello
Working undercover at Christmastime, detective Kevin
Gordon is "hired" to kill a man's ex-wife. Yet the dangerous
thug eludes arrest and is free to stalk Daria Carlisle. Until
Kevin makes it his job to be her yuletide protector.

LISCNMBPA1109